AF350870

UNDERCOVER - Hostages or Slaves?

UNDERCOVER - Hostages or Slaves?

Bob Ojala

Copyright © 2024 Bob Ojala
All rights reserved.
PB ISBN: 979-8-3304-5852-3
EB ISBN: 979-8-3304-8454-6

CONTENTS

Lucy Chavez spent a lot of time at the nice, waterfront hotels along Erie's harbor, where several marinas in the area attracted the singles in town. The boaters came from Detroit, Toledo, and Buffalo to blow off steam for a few days, and the local girls were happy to let them buy them dinner and a few drinks while they were in town.

Occasionally, Lucy was talked into spending the night at one of the luxury waterfront hotels. Her friends said she was asking for trouble, but Lucy told them she only agreed to stay with the nice guys. Tonight was one of those nights.

Lucy walked arm-in-arm with a guy she had just met, up to a nice suite in one of the upper club floors of the Fiesta Bay Hotel. Only the guys with money stayed up there, and this guy had treated her with the utmost respect all evening, including treating her to an expensive dinner.

Lucy was surprised to find three other couples in the room. All three women were Hispanic. It felt unsettling to Lucy because Hispanics were not that common in Erie, and she knew that having four Hispanic women in the same small gathering was not a coincidence. Lucy knew most of the local Hispanic girls in Erie, who were about her age, but she didn't recognize any of these women. The women were dressed a lot flashier than most young girls in Erie would typically dress for a night out on the town.

"Ted, I didn't realize you were having a party," Lucy said to the guy on her arm.

Ted chuckled. "These guys came over from Toledo, They're part of our boating group. I thought you'd like to meet everyone," he responded nonchalantly.

"I just don't like the vibe in the room," Lucy said to Ted. "Where did these girls come from?" "The guys must have found them around the marina, or maybe at the hotel. I didn't ask. What's your problem, Lucy?"

"I don't think these girls speak English. They look confused when your friends talk. Something isn't right here. All of the Hispanics in Erie can speak English, and it looks like these girls can't."

Ted shrugged and walked over to the bar area to order a drink. Lucy surveyed the room as she stood there alone. She felt out of place, and she had a gut feeling that something was off about this "party" Ted had brought her to. Seconds later, she walked over to one of the empty seats next to where the small group was gathered and sat down. One of the girls locked eyes with her, smiled meekly, and quickly looked away. Lucy noticed one of the girls subtly fighting off the man who was trying to nuzzle her neck. The girl soon got up and headed down the hall. Lucy excused herself from the party and followed the girl, whom she assumed was going to the restroom. She got to the door of the single-stall restroom just before the girl locked the door behind her.

The girl looked startled when Lucy quickly entered behind her and locked the door. "Hi, my name is Lucinda," Lucy quickly said in Spanish. "What's your name?"

The girl smiled, almost relieved. "I'm Carmen," she responded in Spanish. "Do you work here too?"

"No. I'm a guest. Are you working for the hotel?"

"Yes. We normally clean rooms at night. Sometimes our boss makes us come to these parties." Lucy nodded. "So, do you live around Erie? Where do you live?" Lucy asked.

"What is Erie?" the girl asked, confused.

"This is Erie, where we are right now," Lucy told her.

A look of panic flashed across the girl's face, and Lucy saw the fear in her expression. "I don't want to get you in trouble, Carmen. I won't tell anyone that we talked, but are you in trouble? Can I help you?"

Carmen looked around the stall, it could barely contain another adult female without feeling too crowded. Who was this woman who had followed her into the bathroom, and what did she want? She had seen her come in with the slender, good-looking American boy, but she still felt like she could trust Lucy.

"I come from Guatemala. They told me if I work here, I can become American citizen. But now, they tell us that we must let these men use us, or they will send us home. We don't know what to do."

Lucy was not surprised. She knew some local prostitutes who did this willingly, but the fact that these girls were being forced made her sick to her stomach. Did Ted believe she was one of them? Is that why he had brought her up to the suite? *Just what was going on?*

Lucy asked Carmen, "Do you want me to get you out of here?"

Carmen looked afraid. She could never leave now. "If I leave, our boss will punish all of us," she said to Lucy.

Lucy took Carmen's hands in hers to assure her that she was there to help. "Where can I find you, to talk to you again, Carmen? I won't just walk away and forget you," Lucy told her, looking straight into Carmen's eyes.

Carmen told Lucy that she and the other girls worked late nights at this hotel. Before Lucy unlocked the door to exit, Carmen warned her to be careful because the men watched them all the time. "Someone may have even seen you come in here behind me," Carmen whispered.

Lucy nodded. Then, unlocking the door and peeking her head out to make sure all was clear, she said to Carmen, "I will find a way to help you and the others. You just try to stay safe, and don't worry about me."

Lucy walked out of the restroom and shut the door behind her. She heard the clicking sound of the lock right before she made her way back to the suite. She walked in to find the guys man-handling the girls. Lucy could see that the girls were not willing, but they were also not objecting. She walked right up to Ted and told him she'd had enough for tonight and was heading home.

Ted became visibly irritated. "Wait a minute. I expected you to stay with me. I bought you dinner and drinks. You owe me!"

"Is that what you expected?" Lucy asked him, anger flashing dangerously in her eyes. Ted took a step back. "I've been known to spend the night with a nice guy, but I can see what you really are, and I'm out of here. Try and stop me if you dare."

Ted slapped Lucy hard across the face. "You Mexican bitch!"

Lucy reacted instinctively by kicking him hard in the groin. Ted doubled over and Lucy stormed out of the room, but not before looking behind her to find Carmen smiling at her. Lucy slammed the door behind her and left.

CHANGING ROLES

Steve and Liz lived in a small, Erie apartment. They intended to find a larger apartment, thinking it was time to start thinking about having a family. However, they were both in the career-growth stage of their lives, so they kept postponing that decision. But ever since they'd been together, they had always de-stressed themselves by discussing the events from their day at work. "You'll never guess who showed up at the shipyard today, asking if Felix and I wanted to have lunch?" Steve started to tell Liz about his day's experiences.

"Not a clue. Give me a hint," Liz answered.

"Looks like a bum on the street corner? Enough of a clue?" Steve said.

"You're kidding! Burt invited you to lunch? I didn't realize that you guys kept in touch."

"Well, he's called me occasionally, just to check up on you. He was concerned about you during that trafficking operation a few years ago. He said he wanted to be sure that you had stopped sticking your neck out."

"So, the two of you have been secretly plotting against me behind my back?" Liz asked, clearly chuckling.

"I wouldn't exactly refer to two guys wanting to keep you alive, as plotting against you!" Steve answered with a wide grin.

"I suppose not. So, what occasion brought about a lunch invitation?" Liz asked.

"Well, Felix and I usually catch lunch away from the ship-yard every couple of weeks, and one day we decided to go over to the hotel on the lakefront. I saw Burt in the restaurant, talk-ing with his friend, the bartender. Burt saw me walk in and came to our table to say hello. I invited him to sit with us."

"When was that? Recently?" Liz asked.

"Oh, maybe two months back. He and Felix hit it off and we discussed the connection this restaurant had with the traf-ficking case where you and Burt met a couple years ago. Felix knew a little bit about that case because of his lady's connec-tions at the Police Department."

"So, today's lunch was just a social occasion?" Liz asked.

"It started that way. Burt wanted to return to the Lake-front Hotel to see some of the friends he'd made there. After the normal chit-chat about you, Felix's lady, and other things, Burt asked me if I would mind him calling you about another trafficking situation he's just found out about. He knows that I worry about you getting too involved in such things."

"I must admit, I do have that tendency," Liz said. "What has Burt found this time?"

"He didn't give too much detail because we were in the restaurant, but I think Fred was suspicious about a situation at the Fiesta Bay, which Burt also knew something about. Fred is the second shift bartender and good friends with the Chief Chef at the restaurant. They've both suspected for some time that many of the Hispanic contractor's staff in the hotel were not just there illegally but may have been brought in by a trafficking operation."

"Talk about role reversal," Liz said. "This is a switch!"

"What do you mean?" Steve asked.

"In the past, if I brought up this subject, you would get hopping mad, telling me it was too dangerous to my emotional health and physical safety," Liz answered with a bit of a sneer.

"It's not that I didn't think those situations weren't important, Liz. I'm just taking your boss's word that he would only use your experience in an advisory role in the future. No more undercover operations. Is that still the deal?"

"It is. So, what did you tell Burt?" Liz asked.

"Burt will call you in your office tomorrow. But please keep me informed about what happens, seeing I'm the one to bring this info to you. Okay?"

"As much as the law allows. I'll keep you updated," Liz said.

Steve had met Liz when one of the captains, a young woman, on one of his father's tugboats stumbled upon a young college girl being kidnapped for a sex-trafficking operation. That lady captain was also kidnapped, and she helped to foil the kidnapping. Liz was working for the Kentucky State Police in their sex crimes unit investigating the case, and Steve became smitten with Liz, who looked much younger than her actual age. From that time forward, Steve had made it a priority in their relationship to keep Liz away from undercover work, which was not only dangerous but causing her emotional issues. Therefore, this was unusual for Steve to even mention the subject, but he had also learned just how pervasive sex trafficking had become in the Midwest, and he knew that his wife was an expert at combating it.

HISTORY

After they got married, Liz and Steve settled into what some might call a "normal" husband/wife relationship. Liz was working as a sex crimes officer with the Kentucky State Police. Liz was 27 but looked like a teenager. She was used in the department's undercover operations She took her job seriously, so the trauma of seeing young kids abducted, drugged, and sold for illicit sex quickly became damaging to her health, both physically and emotionally.

After Liz left the police force, she pursued a law degree and moved to Erie, Pennsylvania, where she became an Assistant District Attorney and Steve worked as a naval architect at the local shipyard.

Two years ago, Liz had gone undercover in a case involving a 13-year-old girl who had been abducted, raped, and held for months in a brothel in neighboring Ohio. That case had also led Liz to work undercover to break up the local sex trafficking operation in Pennsylvania. The pimps were not only using local, abducted victims but also young Chinese and Eastern European children imported to be sold. That undercover operation nearly broke the couple apart when Liz started to head back to her days in Kentucky where she had spiraled into destructive, emotional turmoil.

When the Erie sting was over, Liz promised to leave that undercover role behind. She and Steve had eventually settled down and were even considering starting a family.

Although Steve didn't approve of Liz going back undercover, he was shocked by the young foreign kids being trafficked for sex, and he assisted Liz with locating resources to help relocate the Chinese and Eastern European children to families who could help them overcome the trauma they had been exposed to during their captivity. Because of Steve's compassion, and the help he provided for Liz, she found that she was better able to deal with those emotions, which she was trying to deal with on her own. Although they had very different careers, they had become a team at home, dealing with Liz's unusual work-related problems.

BURT – MORE HISTORY

Burt was ex-FBI and worked with most of the Law Enforcement Agencies in Western Pennsylvania and Eastern Ohio. This meant he was on a first-name basis with many of the field agents. One of them was Sal Dominico, a long-time friend he had worked with in the DEA. Sal eventually went to work with the FBI.

Sal Dominico and Burt had worked together on several joint operations during Burt's time with the FBI and Sal liked Burt's "get 'er done" attitude. However, Sal had warned Burt that his way of doing things would not sit well with the upper echelon of the FBI, and that eventually turned out to be right. Burt sometimes ignored the Rules of Law when he saw a "perp" committing a violent crime. Some of his "collars" resulted in the offender being released by the judge. Burt soon realized that he was not cut out for those Law Enforcement Agencies, and he became an independent private investigator.

When Burt left the FBI, he stayed in touch with Sal, which made it easy for Burt to ask Sal to let him know the next time he was in the Erie area. When Sal said he was scheduled to work an operation in Cleveland, they set a date and met for ribs near Ashtabula. Burt and Sal both liked their Barbeque, and Briquettes Smokehouse was a nice place out near the Lake.

Sal gave Burt a big bear hug when he walked in. They both skipped the beer because of their drives back to Cleveland and Erie, but they ordered a Party Platter with enough barbeque for a small family. When the waiter asked, "What sides do you want?", they both agreed that sides were not why they had come to this place, if the reputation was correct.

"So, Burt. What's this area of concern you're talking about?" Sal said to Burt while biting into a BBQ wing, which they had ordered as an appetizer. "I have fifteen years in the Agency and a wife and kids to support. Is this going to get me fired?"

Burt told Sal about the Majestic Modeling operation that had kept young Chinese children captive as sex slaves for the owner's pedophile customers around Erie. Burt then explained to Sal that he had heard about another type of trafficking involving young Hispanics, mostly women. These women were being brought into the country with promises of citizenship but were ending up being used for labor and sold for sex. Burt asked Sal if he was aware of that operation in this Ohio/ Pennsylvania area.

"I can tell you, Burt, it's not confidential," Sal said, wiping his barbeque-stained fingers on one of the paper towels. "That's an ongoing investigation in the tri-state area. However, the investigation has been tabled, at least for now. No concrete evidence to keep our manpower on it. I'm working on a related investigation with the Bureau of Indian Affairs instead. You're surely aware of all the missing Indigenous kids, both in the U.S. and Canada. They'd been classified as runaways, but the Bureau now believes they've been abducted."

"I heard about the missing Indian kids, yeah. But I also heard the news always referring to them as runaways. If the authorities now realize they're being abducted, it's about time to take it seriously."

"I'm headed to Buffalo next week to get into that case. We believe that many of the abducted Canadian indigenous are somehow crossing the border at that busy, Niagara Falls crossing. But tell me, Burt, what are you hearing about those Hispanic girls? Is that in Erie?"

"Sal, if I can come to you with some solid leads, will the Bureau reopen the investigation which they've tabled?"

Burt knew that he'd have to get some substantial evidence for Sal to convince his boss to reopen their investigation. Sal might want to help, based upon Burt's suspicions, but Sal followed the rules.

"Of course, Burt. We're aware of the casino involvement many of these young Indian girls end up in casinos, but what are you talking about? What's going on in Erie? You don't have casinos there, do you?"

"Not a big casino like elsewhere. I think they call it a Racino, which is a horse track with a casino attached. No hotel like the big casinos."

"So, the Racino is not part of the Tribe-run casinos?"

"No. This one is part of one of the large horse racing groups. But we have many large, waterfront hotels that use large numbers of unskilled laborers, both as night cleaners, maids, and laundry workers. That's where the problem may be happening. I'll do more snooping, but I believe the operation I'm seeing involves maids, cleaners, and other laborers at the local hotels. Does that sound like the same operation you suspect at the casinos?"

"It sounds very similar," Sal said. "When will you have something concrete that I can hand to my Agent-In-Charge? He won't let their investigation continue based only upon suspicions. That's what we have now, and he tabled it."

"I know who to talk to, Sal. His ear is to the ground on all the local dirt, and he always offers to help with stopping the bad guys, particularly traffickers. So, you'll help me, Sal?"

"I will, Burt. But here comes our platter. Let's dig in. I haven't had good barbeque in a while, and this place was highly touted."

Burt enjoyed the barbeque, but he was disappointed that Sal seemed skeptical about his suspicions. Burt understood and knew this was why he didn't fit in with the FBI, following all those rules and protocols.

After dinner, Burt and Sal walked along Ashtabula Harbor, discussing their lives since they had worked together. Sal joked with Burt about buying some nice clothes to replace his shabby exterior, but Burt told him, "Then I'd look like a cop, and people don't divulge secrets to cops!"

"Ooooh! Was that a stab in my back? I thought we were friends?"

"Friends, yes! But I'd never ask you to go along on one of my stake-outs!" Burt responded. "I understand, my friend," said Sal. "That's why I like you."

4

THE PREVIOUS WEEK

Burt had met three young women a couple of years earlier when he was working on a case to catch a child molester. Lucy, Natalie, and Maggie lived on the edge and associated with some friends who occasionally "bent the law" when necessary, they told Burt. The ladies helped Burt with information, and he respected them, but he also knew that they lived a bit closer to danger than he thought they should.

Burt had not spoken to any of those women in two years, so he was surprised when he received a call from Lucy Chavez. "Lucy, what a surprise to see your name pop up on my phone. What a pleasure. What can I do for you?"

"Burt, I remember how you were so willing to help bring that guy to justice a couple years ago. Are you still the sweet, caring guy I remember?" Lucy asked.

"Wow, Lucy! That is the best example of sweet talk I've heard in a long time. I care for people I like, and you are very high on that list. What can I do for you?"

"I think we should meet in person, Burt. I've bumped into something that's upset me, and I don't know what to do about it. I can't just drop it, and I think some nice people are in danger." "Then I'm your guy, Lucy. When and where would you like to meet?"

"Nowhere near the waterfront hotels. What about that place you used to meet that lady lawyer? Some Italian place?"

"Valerio's! Sure, I'd love to meet you there. Just name a day," Burt said.

"Is tonight too soon, Burt? I need to share my concern with someone who can help."

"I can tell that you're upset, Lucy. Tonight works for me. How about 6:30? Do you need a ride?" "No, I can get there. Thank you so much, Burt."

"See you then, Lucy."

Burt was surprised that Lucy had called, but he also knew it had to be something important since she had. Lucy was a beautiful young woman who had inherited all the best looks from her Mexican heritage. Those good looks attracted a lot of guys. Most often, the wrong kind of guys! He also knew Lucy to be a serious person, but she strayed "too close to the flame" as the saying went. Burt would hate to see her get hurt, but knowing the types of people she hung around with, he also knew that was bound to happen someday if she did not distance herself from that crowd.

Lucy met Burt at Valerio's later that night as planned. Burt was already seated at a corner table that provided enough privacy so Lucy could speak freely. Burt had even asked the owner to help keep others away from them for a while, and because the owner knew Burt well, and understood his profession, he had obliged. Every eye turned when Lucy walked into the restaurant and headed directly to Burt's table. When she hugged him, the eyes that had been following her turned from awe to surprise and shock. They all knew Burt, he was occasionally mistaken for a homeless guy, and Lucy was well out of his league.

Burt saw that he was being observed and smiled. "Thank you so much for meeting me so quickly, Burt. I've been upset since Saturday evening, and then I remembered meeting you when that little girl disappeared. You were willing to do any-thing to help catch that guy, even breaking the law if needed. I figured that you'd be the person to help me."

"I wasn't going to break the law if you remember. I was go-ing to plant drugs on the guy's boat. Luckily for all of us, your friends found a better way to solve the problem. So, tell me, what has you so upset now? I owe you, so I hope I can help," Burt said.

Burt asked Lucy if she was in the mood for wine, and Lucy asked for red wine. Burt told the waiter to bring a bottle of Malbec and then asked Lucy to tell him what was bothering her.

"I met a guy on Saturday while I was at the marina. He in-vited me to dinner, and we got pretty friendly. I thought he was a nice guy, so when he invited me to his room, I went. When I got there, there were three other couples, which upset me. But then I also noticed that the other girls were also His-panic, and it appeared that they didn't understand English."

"Very unusual for Erie, isn't it? All about the same age?" Burt asked.

"Yes, having four young Hispanic women at the same party, with no other women there, is almost impossible in this town. They all appeared to be 18-20 years old, maybe even younger. I followed one of the girls into the restroom and she only spoke Spanish. I quickly found out that their boss at the hotel had made them go to the party, and 'to be used' by the men, as Carmen told me. She said she was from Guatemala and had been promised citizenship if she worked at the hotel. I asked her if she wanted to leave with me, but she said they would all be punished. And Burt, when I asked where she lived in Erie, she didn't even know what Erie was. They must be held captive somewhere, unable to communicate with anyone."

"Wow, Lucy. You've really stumbled into a serious situation. You think that all three of those girls were in the same situation?"

"I didn't need to ask them, but it was obvious, Burt. I could tell by their facial expressions that they were not enjoying the situation. They didn't understand much English and they were trying to smile. But I could see that fear was motivating them. They didn't want to be there, and when the men touched them, they stiffened. I felt sorry for them. When I objected, the guy I was with slapped me. My "homie" friends, who you met a couple summers ago, showed me how to stop a guy in his tracks, so after I kicked him, I got out of there."

"We need to do something, but I need to figure out the best approach. You said they were afraid of punishment, so we need to be careful," Burt said.

"I promised Carmen that I wouldn't forget her, and I would try to help her. I wonder how many girls the hotel is using in this way?"

"I know that the hotel uses a contractor for those cleaning jobs. But I wonder if the hotel management is just turning a blind eye to the situation. I hope they really aren't aware, but if I find out that they know, or are being paid to ignore it, I'll find a way for them to be taken down with the contractor."

"I knew you would take this seriously. Thank you so much, Burt. Maybe I can sleep tonight, knowing you're as concerned as I am."

"I think I have the right people to get involved in this, Lucy. I will make a couple phone calls, and I will keep you informed of my progress."

Although Lucy said she wasn't in the mood to enjoy dinner, Burt convinced her to relax and enjoy a small meal with their wine. They both left the restaurant, with Lucy somewhat relieved, and Burt knowing that he would be the one unable to sleep that night. This was probably another form of Human Trafficking, and he had to find help to put an end to it.

A week after he met with Lucy and Sal Dominico, Burt spent an afternoon making his rounds, talking with friends, many of whom were also informants for his private investigations. One of his favorite people was Fred, the night bartender at one of the lakefront hotel restaurants. Fred had helped him break open the trafficking case a couple of years ago. It was during that case that Burt met Liz Trent for the first time, and was introduced to Lucy, by Fred.

Burt walked into the bar where Fred was preparing for work later that night.

"Fred, I'm not working a case on this, but my involvement with that sex-trafficking situation a couple years ago, put me in touch with an old friend who is working with the human trafficking of illegals, mostly Hispanics. He tells me they're lured into the States with promises of citizenship, but end up being used as laborers for the casinos and hotels. Most are used as laundry and night cleaning staff, but some of the young ones are also sold for sex. I was wondering if you'd heard of that occurring in the local hotels?"

"Darn it, Burt. I hadn't put two and two together. I haven't actually heard of that going on here, but I've seen the hotel's labor staff change noticeably from locals to Hispanic women over the last couple years, with maybe a few young guys. I leave my late shift after 2 am, and I walk through the hotel to get to my car. I sometimes see the night cleaners working, but now that you mention it, none of them seem to speak English. When I greet them, they tend to ignore me, and some even turn and walk away from me. I thought they were just shy, but maybe they're afraid that I might suspect they aren't legal."

"I guess we can't be sure that they're part of this trafficking operation, but it sure makes me suspicious. I'm not one of those anti-Mexican, 'wall-builder' fanatics, but if we have illegals being used for slave labor and *sex for sale*, I wouldn't be happy, and I don't want to ignore it," Burt said.

"I share your sentiments on that," Fred said. "Now that you've made me aware of the problem, I'll watch and listen a bit closer. I could call you if anything raises my suspicions further."

"That's great, Fred. As I said, this isn't a job-related inquiry at this point. After what I've seen recently with this trafficking thing, I just can't let it go. So, if you hear anything about the Hispanic labor situation, please call me. If we find anything concrete in our suspicions, I know where to take that information. And you know that I'll keep my sources secret."

After Burt left the bar, Fred asked one of the waitresses to go and find Isadoro. Fred had a question for him. Fifteen minutes later, Isadoro, whom everyone called Izzy, walked into the bar, wiping his hands on a towel. He reached out a hand to shake Fred's hand.

Izzy was a very handsome, Hispanic man, whom all the ladies swooned over. He was married to an Irish woman who would kill him if she ever caught him responding to any of those opportunities. Fred knew him to be a devoted husband and loving father of three young teens.

"I didn't mean to have you come right away, Isadoro. I'm working the late shift," Fred said. "That's fine, Fred, and call me Izzy. Only my mother calls me Isadoro, or Katie when she's mad at me. What can I do for you?"

"Well, first of all, congratulations on the promotion. How does it feel to be the new Executive Chef?" Fred asked.

"After all those years as Sous Chef, I was starting to wonder if it would ever happen. But when Albert retired, he told management they'd lose me if they brought in somebody from the outside. Albert was my biggest cheerleader, so I thank him every chance I get."

"We're all proud of you, Izzy. Glad it happened. But I have a personal issue I want to ask you about if you don't mind."

"No problem, Fred. How can I help?"

Fred explained his connection to Burt and told Izzy about their recent conversation, as well as their mutual concern about trafficking. "Burt understands that I can't jeopardize my job to report anything like this," Fred said to Izzy. "I want to promise you that anything you tell me will not have your name involved. Neither of us wants to lose our jobs. But if you feel the same as Burt and I do about this possible trafficking for slave labor and sex, I'm hoping you might agree to help us expose it, if it's true."

Izzy looked around the bar before responding to Fred. When he did, it was with relief. "Wow, Fred. I've been wondering what to do about this situation. None of my staff in the kitchen are illegals, but I'm pretty sure that some of the contracted workers that come in to clean as we're leaving each night, could be what you describe. They particularly avoid me, because they know that I speak Spanish."

"The aim here is not to send them back. At least neither Burt nor I want that to happen. Though I guess we cannot control what happens."

Izzy nodded. "I know," he said, "my father was a migrant worker in the vineyards. He'd come up every year from Nicaragua. He wanted to stay, but he followed the rules and went home each year. Then he met my mom. She was a sec-ond-generation Mexican American and worked for the vineyard owners as a translator for the migrant workers. They married, so my dad got to stay. He always teased my mom about her probably being illegal. One of these days, I'm going to investigate that to see if Dad was right."

"That's funny," Fred said, laughing softly. "If we uncover an illegal trafficking operation, does that mean we're responsible for deporting some good people?"

"Let me snoop around, Fred. Some of them might rather go home if they're being mistreated here. But my mom also knows a couple good attorneys who work with immigrants, due to her years working with the migrant workers. If we find some deserving people, my mom may be able to help them, if they want to stay."

"That makes me feel better, Izzy. I'm sure that most of these trafficked women are being mistreated by their contractors, but my conscience would bother me if they were deported because of me. My grandfather was technically illegal. He immigrated to Canada from Ireland after the U.S. put a limit on Irish immigrants. My granddad just walked across the border in Maine one night. He eventually married my grandma, and the rest is history, as they say."

"I'm sure there are a lot of those stories in this country. So, let me look into this. I'm friendly with other Hispanics on the hotel staff. I'll ask around and see what they know. Then I'll get back to you and we can decide how to proceed."

"Thanks, Izzy. I'm glad we both feel the same about the situation. But of course, my suspicions could be wrong."

"From the little I've witnessed, Fred, I don't think you're wrong. Your suspicions answered a lot of the questions I've had about some of the workers I've seen here recently."

5

IZZY – MORE SNOOPING

Everyone on the hotel staff liked Izzy, from the hotel manager, right down to the maids. He was like a hero to the young Hispanics who worked on staff at the hotel. Izzy came from an immigrant family and was seen as having succeeded in achieving the '*American Dream*'. The workers loved him because he was a master at code-switching; greeting the Hispanic employees easily in Spanish, and effortlessly switching to English when necessary.

Izzy was on his way home from work one night when he stopped to chat with Emma, one of the older women who managed the maids on the night shift. He saw Emma talking in Spanish to one of the maids outside a guest room, as he took a shortcut through the hotel to his car. He had found a great parking place behind the hotel, much closer than the employee lot.

"Hola, Emma. ~Puedo hacer una pregunta personal?" he asked her.

Emma Kowalski was surprised by Izzy's greeting, but not shocked. Other than simple Spanish greetings, he had never spoken to her in Spanish.

"What's with the Spanish, mi amigo?" she asked him with a small chuckle. "Yes, you can ask me a personal question."

"I'm glad I saw you with nobody else around. This is just between you and me, but have you noticed a lot of empleadas espanolas quien no habla ingles recientemente?"

Emma was silent for a few seconds. Why was Izzy asking her questions about the hotel's Spanish-speaking female employees? "This sounds serious, Izzy. Are we being raided by INS?"

"No, Emma," Izzy chuckled. "This may be worse than just having illegals working here and having immigration officials snooping around. Are you familiar with human trafficking?"

"Yes, I warn my kids and neighbors about it all the time. One of my daughter's young friends disappeared a few years ago. We always wondered if she had been kidnapped by traffickers."

"Maybe we can talk outside of work? Is it possible that some of the contractors' staff might be trafficked from Central America?" Izzy asked Emma.

"Yes. We need to talk. I don't want to get into more details here in the hotel. Maybe we can meet before work tomorrow? When do you come in?"

"I come in at two o'clock. I know you work late tonight. I could stop by your home on my way in. Would about Noon be okay for you?"

"Thank you. That would be nice. I'll have the coffee on," Emma said with a smile.

Izzy was quite worried about how this situation was going to play out. He had decided not to mention his conversations with Fred and Emma to his wife, but Katie noticed his silence during breakfast the next morning. Katie was a serious, red-haired Irish woman who spoke her mind. After their three kids were excused from the table, Katie turned to her husband.

"Okay, my man, what's the problem?" Katie asked her husband while handing him a plate of scrambled eggs and toast. "You're obviously in a funk. Spill it!"

"It's that obvious?" Izzy said, looking lovingly at his wife. "I'm sorry. I hadn't planned on dumping this on you."

"Better that I get dumped on than get the silent treatment. That's way out of character for you." "I guess. But this may be serious."

Katie sat at the table across from her husband and placed a hand over his.

On cue, Izzy continued. "At first, I thought it was just my unfounded suspicion, but last night I spoke with Fred Flynn, one of the bartenders at the hotel. He heard from a customer about some Hispanic women he suspects are being illegally transported and basically used as slave labor. Fred wondered if I had seen any signs of it at our hotel."

"That seems a little far-fetched to me," Katie said. "What did you tell him?"

"Well, I've been wondering about the increase in non-English speaking employees at the hotel, but I hadn't questioned it until Fred mentioned it."

"It still seems hard to believe, though," Katie replied.

"There's more. On my way home last night, I saw Emma Kowalski, the night supervisor for the maids and cleaners. I mentioned my concern to her, and she asked if we could talk away from work. I'm stopping by her home this morning, on my way to the hotel."

"Are you telling me that Emma also believes this is true?" Katie asked.

"She didn't say that, but the fact that she asked to talk away from work makes me think that she knows something."

"If these women are getting jobs that they can't get back home, are you saying we should have them deported? I thought you were sympathetic to immigrants, even the illegal ones."

"Here's the rest of the story, Katie. If Fred's customer's information is correct, then these women are not being paid and are basically slaves, working long hours with only lodging and food as payment. They work for the contractor that supplies the low-skilled positions to the hotel. In addition to that, the young girls are also being sold for sex."

"Oh my God! I've heard of such things in Asia. I didn't think it could happen here."

"I need to see what Emma tells me this morning, and Fred and I cannot be the whistle-blowers, because that would put our jobs in jeopardy. But if this is true, then Fred wants his customer to report the situation to the authorities. Fred said that this customer is well connected with Law Enforcement and can be trusted."

"I know your conscience will guide you, my love. Please let me know what you find out. If this is happening right here, we cannot turn a blind eye to it."

Katie kissed Izzy on his forehead and got up from the dining table. He needed to be on his way to Emma's place before heading to work.

After finishing breakfast with his wife, Izzy left home, pulled into Emma Kowalski's driveway, and stayed in his car. He was fifteen minutes early. A few minutes after he parked, he saw Emma motioning him to come on in.

At 52, Emma Kowalski was starting to, in her words, 'plump out a little'. She was a third-generation Mexican American with dark hair showing a few stray white strands. She was married to a Polish steel worker, and loved by everyone at work and in her neighborhood for her selflessness and generosity. There was not a need that Emma Kowalski could not at least attempt to fill.

She met Izzy on the front stoop of her beautiful ranch-style house and hugged him.

"Can't do that at work, but welcome to my home," she said.

"Thank you for agreeing to meet me. I'm really worried about what may be happening, right under our noses."

"Come in and have some coffee. We do need to talk."

Izzy followed Emma inside the house through the front door and to the back of the house, into the kitchen. Emma pulled out a seat at the kitchen table, cleared the pile of used dishes, and asked Izzy to sit. "Sorry for the mess, Izzy. My husband just left for the factory about thirty minutes ago. I didn't have a chance to clean up before you arrived."

"Not a problem, Emma. Our crazy hours at work make a normal life difficult. So, what do you think, Emma? Is this situation really going on at the hotel?" Izzy asked, as soon as he was seated.

Emma walked towards Izzy with two mugs of coffee in her hands. "When you asked me last night, it hit home right away. I've been suspecting something wasn't right." Offering a mug to Izzy, she continued, "I always had a few new girls that spoke minimal, broken English. But starting maybe a year and a half ago, the lack of English has steadily gotten more prevalent. Now, nearly all of the girls who come from the contractor speak little or no English." Emma sat down in the seat next to Izzy and took a sip of her coffee. "My Spanish is not as great as it was before my mom died. My kids identify as being Polish, so I haven't had to use my Spanish much until this started happening. So, tell me, what do you think is happening?" Emma asked.

Izzy told Emma what Fred had told him. Again, he asked Emma, "Could it be true?"

"Well, let me tell you a few things I've noticed. It occasionally happened in the past that one of the girls came in with a black eye or a cut lip. I'd hear the girls talking about it during their breaks, with bravado in their voice, usually about a fight with a boyfriend. But this last year or so, most of those new girls have come to work with signs of violence, particularly when they first started. These girls never talk about it or bad-mouth a boyfriend, like the girls did in the past. They seem to be very sullen and quiet when it happens. What really worries me is the real young, pretty ones. I see them missing work quite often. When I ask where they are, the others tell me, 'woman problems', but when they come back to work, I see the others trying to console them."

"I think I know where that is leading. Am I right?" Izzy asked.

"Yes. At first, I thought it was a boyfriend having sex with them. But now I've seen it happen often enough, and the girls all gather around her, consoling her. Sometimes there are tears shed during those sessions, very unlike the past."

"So, we are both suspecting the same thing," Izzy said, "that these girls have been raped."

"That's what I think. And if it happened once or twice, I guess rapes are becoming more common. But I have seen this at least a dozen times. That's too common to be just a few un-lucky girls. I was worried before, but now I'm convinced that someone at that agency is selling them for sex. And if your sus-picion about the slave labor is correct, we need to do some-thing."

"I agree. I'll ask Fred to contact his customer and ask what we should do. If he can keep our names out of it, maybe we can tell him what we've experienced."

"Yes, Izzy. We cannot have this information and do noth-ing about it."

"Thanks, Emma."

When Izzy left Emma's home and drove to work, he felt a sick feeling in his stomach. Izzy had a teenage daughter, and he realized how traumatic a rape would be. How will these young women ever be able to return to a normal life after being abused in a foreign country, and unable to ask for help?

6

WHAT TO DO?

A few days after his brief conversation with Izzy, Fred called Burt to tell him he had some information on the possible trafficking operation at the hotel. He then arranged to meet with Emma, Izzy, and Burt at Emma's house that Saturday morning. Emma had suggested it as a meeting place because she thought meeting there would raise the least suspicion.

Before they all got together, Burt asked if a young woman named Liz Trent could attend the meeting. He told them Liz had a lot of personal experience with trafficking, and that she could be trusted, but he did not tell them that Liz was an Assistant District Attorney.

Burt also called Tom Pierson, the District Attorney, and asked about the status of the FBI's investigation into the trafficking at the casinos and hotels. He and Tom had become friends after being hired for investigative work by the DA's office.

"At our weekly inter-agency meeting last Monday, the FBI said they have no further leads. They are about to table the active investigation. Why do you ask, Burt?"

"I may have found some witnesses to that activity. However, the job security and safety of those witnesses is my responsibility. I know that this currently isn't your responsibility, but I need some experts on trafficking to help me talk to these witnesses. Can..."

"I know what you want to ask, Burt. Officially, the answer is, no! But what my assistants do in their free time is up to them, as long as they don't involve my office."

"Understood. Thanks, Tom," and Burt hung up the call.

Later that evening, Burt called Liz Trent after working hours.

"I understand you called my boss," Liz said when she answered the phone. "He said if you call me, I was not to mention it to him. What on earth is this all about?"

"Tom is a great guy. Covering his bases beforehand. Can we meet to talk over a problem, which you cannot talk about with anyone, particularly your boss?" Burt asked.

"Of course. When do you want to meet? Do I assume this is the subject you discussed with Steve at lunch recently?"

"Yes, but I think it's best if Steve doesn't know any more about this right now. Okay?" "Steve is getting used to being excluded from these discussions. No problem."

"Seeing this has to be done in your free time, is Saturday okay for you?" Burt asked. "I hate to impose on your free time with Steve."

"Saturday works fine. Steve has some special event at the shipyard on Saturday, whatever a launching means. What's your plan?" Liz responded.

"I want you to meet some great people at ten on Saturday morning. Can I pick you up at nine, so I can explain what's happening? I'll supply the large Americanos."

"I was ready to say I need my beauty sleep, but the Americanos got me hooked. I'm looking forward to seeing you again. What's it been? Six weeks?"

"What? Feeling withdrawal? See you Saturday. Give my regards to that guy of yours."

Liz had worked with Burt two years ago when she went undercover to investigate a local modeling agency that was using their young models for sex. Burt started out doing surveillance work for the DA, tracking the modeling agency's owner to where he was hiding some foreign kids. But when Burt saw that Liz was possibly in harm's way, he also became her protector. Their respect for one another continued ever since.

When Burt pulled up to Liz's apartment that Saturday, Liz was already sitting on her apartment stairs. She hopped into the beat-up Lexus that Burt was driving and looked around before closing the equally beat-up door.

"Another Sherriff's auction special, I assume?" she said, turning to look at Burt.

Burt smiled.

"And where's the Americano you promised?" she added.

Burt reached into the back seat and handed Liz her Americano. "Just picked up this beauty last week," he said referring to the car. "A drug dealer lost control in a high-speed chase.

Got the car for $500, and the headlights and alignment only cost me $1800. The dents in the fenders lend character, so I'm driving a Lexus for $2300. I would have preferred a Mercedes, but these young drug dealers have no real class."

"You're too much, Burt," Liz said, laughing. "Nice interior though. So, tell me, what's our meeting all about?"

"First thing, the people we're going to meet this morning could lose their jobs or be in danger if their cooperation is revealed. I know you can be trusted not to reveal their names, but I need to be sure you understand. Okay?"

"Okay, Burt."

"When I last spoke with your boss, I asked what he knew about the FBI's investigation into the trafficking at the casinos and hotels."

"The word around the office this week was that it dead-ended. Tabled until further leads come in," Liz said. "But seeing you've brought it up, do I assume you know something I do not?"

"Am I that transparent?" Burt said, laughing. He then went on to tell Liz about his conversation with Fred, and the two hotel employees who believed that both slave labor and sex trafficking were occurring in at least one of the local hotels. Burt had suggested having an expert on human trafficking at the meeting. "But remember, Liz, they cannot know you work in the D.A.'s office. It might be better if I just refer to your previous experience in Kentucky."

"I think that's a good idea. If it comes up, I can just say I moved here with my fiancé." "Well, you've married the guy now, but we don't need to mention that."

"He used to ask me a couple times a week, Burt. I was just getting tired of telling him that I'd think about it."

"You just terrorized that poor young man, Liz. You never would have found anyone who wanted you more than Steve."

"I know that, Burt. Steve wasn't the problem. Until that Chinese trafficking sting, I was worried that I would make his life miserable with my moods. When I'm working on a heart-wrenching case, I get so involved in it that I take it home with me. During that sting operation, and then working with those young Chinese and Moldovan kids, I was so emotional, I thought I'd snap. But Steve saw it happening and he helped me through it. I had always kept those problems inside, but Steve talked me through that dilemma, even suggesting people to call and how to talk to the kids who knew some English. I then came to realize that Steve could be part of my life and that my problems didn't upset him, as long as I included him in the process."

"You've got a keeper there, Liz. I was so happy when you two got married. I was sorry I couldn't get out to Chicago for the wedding."

"Maybe down the road, Steve can help you with this one as well, but for now, I've promised Tom, without actually saying it, that you're not to involve his office," Burt said.

"I'm ready, Burt. Let's see what these people know."

When Burt and Liz arrived at Emma's house, Fred was already there. After settling in Emma's airy living room, Fred introduced Burt and Liz to Emma and informed them that Izzy was on his way. They would dive into the deeper conversation once Izzy arrived, but for now, they chatted about kids and grandkids.

They soon heard a car pull up in Emma's graveled driveway and Emma stood up to go and meet Izzy at the door. Emma greeted Izzy with a hug, then she walked him into the living room and introduced him to the others. Fred told Emma and Izzy that Burt was the customer who first brought his attention to the possibility that they had trafficking going on at their hotel. Then, turning to Liz and Burt, he continued, "Burt, I've just met this young lady, so, I'll let you explain why you requested that she attend our meeting."

Burt sat forward in his seat and began to speak. "I recently met Liz Trent and thought she was some young girl not able to legally buy a beer. But I soon learned she was 30 years old and retired from a nerve-wracking career as a Kentucky State policewoman, working undercover on sex crimes, human trafficking in particular. I thought her expertise would be important, both to determine if we are dealing with a trafficking ring at the hotels and if so, how we can proceed while protecting the three of you. Liz understands that your jobs and your safety are at stake here, and I trust Liz to keep your identities secret. Because of her background, she would know who to call, and she can be the whistle-blower, thus keeping you all out of it."

Emma and Izzy told Liz and Burt why they became suspicious and were worried that there was a trafficking operation at their hotel. They tried to give Liz as many details as they could, including the conversations Emma had overheard between the girls on her staff. They asked Liz if she thought there could potentially be trafficking, or if she thought they were just being paranoid.

"Everything you've told me adds up to trafficking," Liz said, "particularly the girls you think were raped. Rape victims seldom report it, but when trafficked girls are sold for sex, they are threatened with physical violence, or with being sent back home if they object. Some might wish they could go back home, but they now feel like their bodies have been violated and life back home would never be the same. After repeated sex, they just give up. So, I'm quite certain you have a contractor who is using trafficked people as his employees. But let me ask you this, Emma, is there at least one girl who seems more in control? She probably never cries with the others, and the younger girls seem afraid of her?"

Emma looked questioningly at Izzy, and then Fred, before responding. "Yes, that would be Lily. She started about the time I noticed the change in employees."

Liz was nodding. "She's like the house mother," she said. "American pimps call that girl 'the bottom'. It's a weird phrase because they are actually at the top of the chain. She may be sold for sex as well, but the head of the trafficking organization treats her like she is the one he likes. So, to keep the pimp happy, she spies on the other girls and reports back to him."

Emma's hands flew up to cover her mouth. "Oh my God," she said, "I had no idea people could be like this. Now that you describe it, I have seen the reactions of some girls towards Lily. She must be terrible."

"Don't blame Lily," Liz said. "She suffered through the same humiliations and violence as the others, but now she's been broken. She also cooperates out of fear, but if their pimp, or head of the organization treats her just a little better than the others, she continues to do as she is told to keep his occasional favors. That may just be better meals or an occasional new dress. This is why trafficking is such a terrible thing. When Lily gets too old or loses her appeal to the Johns, she'll be tossed out, or possibly even killed. The pimps treat them as possessions, not as people."

"So, what do we do now?" Izzy asked.

"You don't do anything. I still have my contacts in the FBI, and I'll tell them I overheard some girls talking while at the hotel for a meeting. My high school Spanish isn't too good, but I can report what I overheard. The FBI will take it from there. Do you have an estimate of how many girls the contractor has, just at your hotel?"

"I have twelve girls that work for me in housekeeping," Emma said. "I think I've seen five more in Laundry, and Izzy thinks they are using some to clean his kitchen a night. And by the way, Izzy and I are worried about all these girls being sent back home. We hate to feel responsible for them being deported. Is there anything we can do to help them?"

"I'm sure that some may be deported. But I know someone in the INS Office in Pittsburgh. I'll ask him if he can treat each case individually. If the girls can show that their life would be in danger if they return home, or other serious issues, the INS may consider them for asylum."

"If you can give us some warning about when things may happen, my mother has a few friends who are immigration attorneys. Maybe she can ask them to help the more deserving girls that want to remain here," Izzy said.

"I'll certainly ask to be kept in the loop, and then I can notify you. And yes, your mother's attorney friends may certainly get involved, and be very helpful."

Burt then added, "I also want you to be aware of another active FBI investigation, concerning the large number of Indigenous kids that go missing from the U.S. and Canadian Tribal Reservations. They had always been classified as runaways by the Bureau of Indian Affairs, but the FBI has found that many of them have been abducted. Please keep your eyes and ears open for those girls, if you would. My friend at the FBI is involved with that investigation."

Emma, who had been listening intently to the discussion, said, "Is there no end to the abuse that's inflicted on our Native population? Thank you for telling us about that, Burt. I'm sure we will watch for any signs of that as well."

The group sat for a while, getting to know a few life-details about one another. Then, all of a sudden, Emma spoke up: "Now that I've had a chance to know our guests better, Liz and Burt, I consider you my new friends, and I believe I can trust you," Emma said. "I now need to admit that I know more about what is happening than I have been telling you. This has bothered my conscience ever since it happened, and I need to tell you."

"You can trust Burt and me," Liz said. "Feel free to tell us, and we promise to keep the information confidential. The last thing we want to do is to get you into trouble or to jeopardize your job or your safety."

Emma continued, "About six months ago, one of my cleaners didn't show up for work, which is very unusual. They work hard and always show up. I asked one of the girls who I knew she was friendly with, and the girl said she was hurt. I asked if it happened at work, thinking I needed to file an injury report. But her friend began crying, telling me that the injured girl had been told to attend a party after work with two other girls. When the three girls returned, around 2 AM, they were frantic, waking up all the others in the wing where they were sleeping. One of the girls was bleeding seriously, and they said it was vaginal bleeding. Her friend said that she was not at that party, but the other girls said that when the injured girl objected to sex, the men had gang-raped her until she passed out. Then the men got scared and called the hotel staff to take the girls away."

"Oh my God," Liz said. "This is just what I was afraid could be happening. Is she okay? Did she get medical help?"

"No. I asked the girls, and they said that a woman named Lydia had come and told the other girls to go to bed. Lydia made a phone call, and a van came to where they were staying and took the girl away. They never saw her again. Then, a few days later, when the two other girls who were with her at the party started to ask where their friend was, they were picked up in a van and never returned to where they slept. They've also disappeared. I don't know if that injured girl survived but based upon the description I got from the other two, I think she could have died without immediate medical care."

Emma started crying and both Liz and Izzy went over to comfort her. Then Emma said, "I should have called someone, but the person who the girls said had organized that sex party is one of the Assistant Managers at the hotel, so I was afraid. Now I believe that I could be responsible for that girl's death, and who knows what they did to those other two girls."

Liz said, "By the time you realized that the girl had been hurt, Emma, she had already been taken away. In three-days-time, there was nothing you could have done."

"But I should have reported it, not ignored it."

"No, Emma. You see, this organization got rid of the other two girls who tried to find out what happened to her. The type of people we are dealing with here would have found a way to silence you as well. I know you feel bad, but for your and your family's welfare, I'm glad you didn't report it. Now it is up to the people I know to investigate this. So, if you know the name of the man who organized that sex party? Can you tell me his name? And again, I will not divulge my source."

Emma looked over at Izzy, looking for advice. Izzy said, "Yes, Emma. You need to tell Liz. I can leave if you'd rather not name him with me in the room."

"I just hesitated, Izzy, because I know you consider this man a friend. But I think you need to know. It is Duncan, the hotel's Banquet Manager."

"Wow!" Izzy said. "I never would have guessed. But since his divorce a couple of years ago, he has not been the same. He's changed a lot."

"The cause could be the need for extra money, Izzy. I'm sure he was offered a cut of the income from selling the girls," Liz said. "I'm sure the investigators will be checking on him closely. He may have been the one who picked up the injured girl and also the other two. Hopefully, the investigation will find out what happened to them."

As Liz and Burt drove away from the meeting, Liz said, "Here we are again, Burt. We always seem to work together under these terrible circumstances."

Burt replied, "That's our role in life, Liz. We seem destined to help people in trouble. I feel great satisfaction in finding the bad guys, and it's your job to prosecute them. I also find ways to punish those guys that get away."

"I'm not sure that I want to know about how you do that, do I?" Liz asked.

"Probably not!" Burt said.

7

DISTRICT ATTORNEY'S
OFFICE

A week later, Burt called Liz at her office. He wanted to know if the FBI was interested in what Liz now knew about the hotel employees."

"Oh yes! I told Tom that we needed to update the FBI about the situation," Liz said to Burt. "He

did that at Monday's inter-agency meeting. Tom asked me to contact you and ask if you could meet with the FBI Agent in charge of that investigation. Some guy named Sal, but I don't remember the last name."

"No kidding! Fantastic! Sal is an old friend from my FBI days," Burt responded excitedly.

Liz smiled on the other end of the line. "That's great, Burt!" she said. "Now that they have the name of the contractor supplying workers to that hotel, they can expand their investigation." "Yes, that's right," Burt said.

"Until this lead, they only had a few illegals working at a Casino in Ohio. They couldn't link them to an organized trafficking ring, so your information will hopefully help to break it wide open."

"I'm glad this might stop the trafficking, Liz, but I'm worried about how those non-citizens will be handled by the FBI. Deporting them, particularly those who were sold for sex, will be terrible for them."

Liz paused to wave back at her colleague who was walking by her open office door. Then she continued. "Tom did ask that question of the Cleveland Agent who attended that meeting yesterday, and he promised that each case would be handled individually. He told us that two of the women in that Ohio casino raid were granted political asylum. The third woman wanted to go home. He did mention that none of those three had been sold for sex, however. They were unpaid laundry workers, supplied by a local man in Cleveland, who had at least ten other laborers living in an old house. He used them to fill contracts he had to clean office buildings, as well as those laundry workers."

Burt sighed deeply. "This is another side to this trafficking situation, which I hadn't realized until recently. With all the countries around the world in trouble, I guess these traffickers will prey on anyone trying to flee their poverty situation. Sex-slave or labor-slave, these unscrupulous people will use them. Once they're here, they're afraid to complain and they have nowhere to run."

"All we can do is be vigilant, Burt. In this case, our office had no connection to these types of operations or trafficked victims, until that local, Majestic Modeling situation a couple years ago. However, with our connections to the other agencies, please feel free to contact Tom or me when you find things like this. I know that I cannot be the undercover person on this one. My Spanish-speaking skills barely suffice at a Mexican restaurant. It's going to be tough gathering evidence. Even Emma would be unable to see and hear what we will need in order to get the necessary evidence on the traffickers."

Burt agreed, but he had an idea on how to solve that problem and promised Liz that he would get back to her."

When Liz got home later that evening, Steve pressed her for information about what he now termed the "Latina trafficking at the hotels?"

"Are you spying on me, or have you talked to Burt today?" Liz asked him, teasing.

"I'll take that to mean something happened today. I knew your boss had his inter-agency meeting on Mondays, so I wondered what the status was with that situation," Steve said.

Plopping herself on the couch to take off her shoes, Liz told Steve about her earlier conversation with Burt in her office. "From what Burt and his friends provided, the FBI investigation has found two contractors who are importing women from Central America. We're not directly involved at the D.A.'s office, but Tom's inter-agency meetings implied that they've re-opened that investigation. It looks like the FBI could be making arrests soon at the contractor's two Cleveland locations."

"I know everyone was worried about deporting those women. Do you know how that will be handled?" Steve asked. He was now sitting on the edge of the coffee table rubbing Liz's feet.

Liz leaned back onto the sofa and relaxed. "Burt's friend's mom knows the local immigration attorneys. He will start to gather information on each of the women as they are identified. The goal is to see if they qualify for asylum status. Those attorneys are going to contact INS and they will prepare an evaluation of each woman's case individually. Nearly half of the women they have rescued in their Cleveland raids have opted to go back home. I think their impression of life in the United States has been soured by the treatment they received," Liz said.

"Is this going to result in more work outside of your real job at the D.A.'s office? You did a great job with those Chinese kids and the Moldovan teens. Is your boss going to have you working with these Latinas?" Steve continued.

Liz put her foot down and sat up. "Well, to put your mind at ease, my boss preempted any undercover work on my part if that is your concern," she said, looking into Steve's eyes. Then she stood up and walked towards the kitchen. Steve followed. "Burt is meeting with his FBI friend tomorrow to discuss what information he and his friends at the hotel have uncovered. Burt promised those hotel employees that their names wouldn't be used at this time. Once the case becomes public, however, their testimony may be required. I know that Burt thinks that an undercover person may be helpful in the investigation, but I suspect that my high school Spanish and blond hair won't be very convincing."

"That's fine with me," Steve said, his arms folded as he leaned against the door frame. He also suggested a few places where the rescued girls could stay when they were freed from the traffickers.

"Will that place you found for the Moldovan and Bulgarian girls be willing to help again? Do they have any Spanish-speaking staff?" he asked.

"I need to ask my boss if he'll allow me to get involved with this part of the situation. After all, I'm an Assistant DA, not a counselor, as you often remind me. But knowing Mr. Pierson as I do, I'm sure he'll allow me some time to work on getting help for the rescued girls."

"Maybe that girl you rescued on the last sting? The one who works for the women's shelter?" Steve suggested.

"That's certainly one great possibility," Liz said, "but she is not a Spanish speaker. I'm hoping she has made some good contacts since then, who have Spanish-speaking skills."

"That's good," Steve responded. "I would hate to see those girls rescued and not have a plan in place to help them. They're going to be traumatized when this thing happens."

"There you go again, my love. You hate seeing me worry about these people, but you are taking over in the worrying department."

"It's just that …," Steve began.

"No, Steve. I understand and I love you for being this way. You can't imagine how helpful you were two years ago, offering suggestions to those Chinese and Moldovan kids. Because I knew you were as concerned as I was, it relieved the pressure I usually felt in those situations. I want you to offer help with ideas again this time. Thank you …"

Liz was unable to finish speaking because Steve pulled her into a wonderful embrace.

8

BURT CONTACTS LUCY

Burt called and asked to meet with Lucy a few days later, following his very productive meeting with Emma, Izzy, and Fred. He wanted to update her on the progress he had made since it was her concern that got the ball rolling.

Lucy was thrilled to know that something was going to be done about her concerns. She asked Burt if he had time for a home-cooked dinner, and it was Burt's turn to be excited. Lucy said that she had confided in her two girlfriends, Maggie and Natalie, about what she had witnessed at Fiesta Bay Hotel. She wanted to know if it was okay with Burt if she invited them to dinner also.

"Are you sure they can keep this info under wraps? We have people's jobs and lives in our hands here," Burt asked her, a little hesitant about allowing other people into the know of what was going on. "You've already met these girls. They're street people, and they've spent their lives keeping secrets. If you describe the situation to them in that way, I would trust them with my own life."

"I remember them well, and if you trust them, then I do as well. When do you want to get together?"

"Let me call Mag and Nat to see if they are busy, but I'm thinking about tomorrow. Is 4 o'clock okay for you? That would give us time to talk while dinner is getting ready."

"That sounds perfect. Let me know if your friends can make that work."

Two hours later, Lucy had confirmed the meeting with Burt for the next afternoon, and that Maggie and Natalie were looking forward to seeing Burt again.

Burt remembered Maggie and Natalie. They had helped him "nail" a spoiled, rich guy preying on underage girls a few years ago. The "dazzling trio" as Burt thought of them, was a mix of three beautiful young girls: Natalie was black, Lucy was Hispanic, and Maggie was a fiery, red-headed Irish girl. Because they went to high school together and had similar family histories, including lack of money and luxuries, they could care less about their varied racial differences, and they became close, lifelong friends. They were in their early 20s and had all come from working-class homes. They were also extremely street-smart. They had friends who dabbled in petty crime, but the girls kept themselves clean, as far as any criminal activity was concerned.

Burt worried that "using rich guys" was more dangerous than the three women realized. He liked them and worried about their safety.

The next afternoon, Burt arrived at Lucy's apartment a few minutes early. Lucy greeted him at the door and invited him in. Natalie and Maggie were on their way.

Burt had never been to Natalie's apartment, so he was a bit shocked to see the nice furniture, art, and tasteful decor. None looked to be extremely expensive, but it was more than he had expected to see.

"Not what you expected?" Lucy asked Burt, having noticed him looking around. "Just impressed by your tastes, I guess."

"Well, they're all mine, though many of them were gifts from friends. I know that you worry

about my lifestyle, but I like nice things, and I accept gifts from my admirers. I hope you understand."

"I understand, but I like you and I worry about you. Just like the guy you met at the hotel at that party. His intentions were not good, and you were lucky not to be hurt."

"Thanks, Burt. I'm happy that you worry about me, but I hope you don't judge me poorly. It's just that I like nice clothes and trinkets, and my retail sales salary can't buy them all. I'm young and men find me attractive. Maybe I'm using them, but I never ask for money. When they offer gifts, I accept that. Do you understand?"

"I certainly understand, Lucy. And I'm not judging you as a person. I think you are a wonderful, caring person. If you weren't, you'd never have come to me about the welfare of those girls you saw at the hotel. But I like you and I do worry about your safety."

Lucy was about to answer when there was a knock at her door. Lucy leaned forward and kissed Burt on the cheek before answering the door and letting Maggie and Natalie in. After exchanging hugs with Lucy, the three ladies turned to

Burt and each hugged him. "Wow, Burt! You dressed up for the occasion," Natalie said to Burt teasingly. "When I see you around town occasionally, it always looks like you're dressed for some undercover operation."

"Well, that is the type of work I do, you know. I just call it 'blending into the crowd'."

"Hey, Nat! Don't give Burt a hard time. He has always dressed nicely when he meets with us. Maybe he's mistaken us for the upper class. We should feel complimented," Maggie said, laughing.

Pointing to the four chairs around her glass-top dining table, Lucy welcomed them to sit. "I'm just happy we have this guy as a friend. When we see things we can't handle, Burt always knows what to do," Lucy said. "Although last time, we did need to point out that his plan of planting drugs on that guy would never work."

"That's why I'm here to see you ladies," Burt said, taking a seat. "We have another situation that needs some covert actions, and we need to discuss possible solutions."

"Did you hear that, girls?" Maggie quipped. "Burt called us 'ladies', so watch out."

Lucy answered, "What I like about Burt is that he does think about us as ladies. Our neighborhood friends still see us as some of the girls, but Burt gives us more credit than that. So, shall we open a bottle of wine and talk over this latest problem? I just put dinner in the oven, and it should be ready in 45 minutes."

"I assume we are discussing the situation you witnessed at the hotel with those three young women who didn't speak English?" Natalie asked.

"Yes, that's it," Lucy said. "Burt has followed up on that information and wanted to bring me up to date. But Nat and Mag, Burt has confided that what he has to tell us could endanger some people's lives, and certainly have them lose their jobs, so I promised Burt that our lips are sealed. I explained to him that our lives in the old neighborhood always involved secrets, so we all know how to keep our mouths shut."

Both Natalie and Maggie nodded. "Not a problem, Burt."

Lucy pulled out the chair nearest to the kitchen and sat down. "As I had told you girls soon after I was taken to that hotel party, the three women in that room were not happy," Lucy said. "They were not there by choice, and they were not prostitutes. I confirmed that by talking with one of them in the restroom. The situation worried me enough that I called Burt, and Burt promised to look into it. Less than a week afterward, Burt called to update me. So, that is the purpose of this meeting, to see what he has discovered."

Burt told the ladies about his meetings with Sal Dominico and the hotel's employees, and that Lucy's suspicions had been confirmed after several of the employees shared their experiences. What Lucy discovered, certainly appeared to be trafficked Hispanic women being used for slave labor, and illicit escort services.

"Is this just going to be a raid to have these girls deported?" Natalie asked.

"Not at all," Burt reassured them. "My contact at the FBI promised that he will work with INS to handle each case on a one-on-one basis. The last trafficking ring we busted here in Erie involved both Chinese kids and Eastern European teens. All of the Chinese kids were eventually adopted by Chinese-American families. Even the adults who were trafficked to care for them were placed in a Chinese Community Center down in Pittsburgh. I know the Eastern European teens were not deported, but I'd have to ask where they were placed. All of those kids were orphans and had no place to go if sent back."

"That's good," Natalie said. "If I thought we were just sending them back to poverty, I'd be very against helping."

"My contact said that a couple of the women they rescued in Cleveland recently had opted to return to Mexico. But those women were only used as laborers and were not sold for sex. From what I heard at my meeting with the hotel employees, they think the sexual abuse has traumatized some of these young girls. He said that INS is surprisingly sympathetic towards people who have been trafficked, even though these women came here believing they would become American citizens."

"How are they going to break this up and get the contractors arrested?" asked Maggie. "I know they can't just walk into their office and accuse them. It's not like the Police or the FBI will just take the word of these girls, will they?"

"That's where it becomes tough. If you remember from a couple years ago, when we worked on stopping that yachter guy, we were lucky to have an experienced, retired sex crime officer who went undercover to find the evidence we needed.

I had that lady at this meeting with the hotel workers and she expressed the need to have someone working on the inside. We didn't discuss details, but obviously, it would have to be a young, Spanish-speaking woman, either working in the hotel or for that contractor."

Before Burt could go any further, both Natalie and Maggie looked at one another and then turned toward Lucy.

"Now wait a minute! I'm not a trained investigator, and I have a job. I can't just quit my job."

Maggie leaned forward across the table and looked directly at Lucy.

"But Luce, you always tell us how your boss keeps telling you to take a nice, long, vacation. You're the one who asked Burt to find a way to help these women, so here's your chance. Come on Burt, don't you think Lucy could do this?"

"In fact, I do," said Burt. "I was actually hoping that Lucy might volunteer. She's the right age, she speaks Spanish. And at least one of those girls already trusts her. The team I'm working with can train her on any investigative skills she needs, and if she gains the trust of some people in the trafficking operation, she can wear a 'wire' for us to get the necessary incriminating evidence. I don't want to force you, Lucy, but what do you say?"

Lucy was silent for a long time as Burt and her friends just stared at her.

"Can I talk to your FBI guy and hopefully someone from INS as well?" Lucy said, sighing heavily. "I want to see how this can work out. I don't want to put these young women in danger, and I also want to hear how INS will protect them afterward."

"I'm sure that can be arranged," said Burt. "I know you met the young lady who worked undercover on the last sting operation. I'll contact her to see if she could meet with you to answer some of your concerns. Once we get a go-ahead from the FBI team, I will also have you meet the hotel staff who suspected this was happening. I think that once you meet everyone, you will feel comfortable, knowing they all have your back, and they have the best interests of those women. The agents who work with trafficked people are very concerned with both their rescue and providing counseling. They have learned to hate the traffickers for their total lack of humanity."

"Okay, Burt. Please arrange those meetings. If I like what I hear, then I'll help in any way that I can." Then looking at Natalie and Maggie, Lucy said, "If I lose my job, which one of you is going to take me into your apartment?"

Natalie and Maggie stood up and hugged Lucy. Then together, they happily chatted their way into the kitchen.

"Ladies, let me excuse myself to make a few phone calls," Burt said, looking over his shoulder as he rose from the chair and headed towards the balcony. "I need to see if I can arrange these meetings."

"Well don't take too long. Dinner will be out of the oven soon. Mexican chicken casserole, with stuffed Mexican peppers. My mom's recipes."

When he met with Liz a few days earlier, Burt had not mentioned the idea of Lucy going undercover because he wasn't sure how Lucy would react to the idea at the time.

Now that he knew she might be okay with the idea, Burt wanted Liz to comment on it and maybe propose the idea to the FBI team. Burt didn't foresee any danger for Lucy if she was just gathering information.

Burt explained the situation to Liz and she said she would bring up the suggestion during a meeting her office was having with the FBI team the following day. "I'll tell them about your idea, and if they believe it will work, I'm sure they may want to meet this woman," Liz told Burt. "Can you find out if she's available to meet with them? And, please tell Lucy that I am proud of her willingness to get involved."

Burt didn't want to tell Liz that it was probably only due to the urging of Natalie and Maggie that Lucy was considering this, instead, he just asked Liz to warn the FBI agents that Lucy had some concerns. "She does not want to be part of this if the women will just be gathered up and deported," Burt said to Liz. "I assured Lucy that INS would handle each of them on a one-on-one basis. Can you arrange for Lucy to meet with the INS agents to discuss that issue? And also, how will these women be handled once they are rescued? Do we have a Spanish-speaking organization in the area where the women can be housed and counseled?"

Liz answered, "I like Lucy's attitude, Burt. Her concerns are very relevant, but if we found a way to work with the Chinese and Moldovan abductees in that Majestic Modeling sting, I'm sure we can find a similar solution for these women. Finding Spanish-speaking help should be much easier than Chinese and Moldovan translators. Let me ask my boss if he will add Lucy to the meeting agenda, and if we can add the

INS Agent from Pittsburgh to the meeting. If they're not available on such short notice, you can assure Lucy that I will be sure her concerns are addressed."

"Thanks, Liz. I think you met Lucy briefly a couple years ago when I was tracking down that guy luring the young girls out on his yacht. I don't think you got to know her very well back then, but she has a passion as strong as yours, and she is attracted to people who are in trouble. You'll like Lucy."

"I remember her. I do look forward to getting to know her better. And thanks for the compliment, Burt."

"Well, you know I'm the President of the Liz Trent Fan Club! Your husband is Chairman of the Board."

"I'll tell Steve about his honorary title. Thanks, Burt."

9

MEETING THE TEAM

Liz knocked on Tom Pierson's door after talking with Burt. Tom was the district attorney. He looked up from his work and, seeing Liz, motioned her into his office and pointed at the chair across from him while pointing at his phone and raising his index finger. Liz planted herself in the chair and waited.

A minute or two later, Tom hung up the phone. "That was my oldest daughter. She's making college visits with my wife next week, and she wanted to ask if the University of Chicago was worth visiting. I told her that other than the cost of tuition, it was a great school. I thought that girls in High School were expensive, but the cost of tuition has skyrocketed since I was in college."

"Is she going into Law? As you know, I think highly of my alma mater, Michigan."

"She at least seems to want to study the prerequisites for Law as an undergrad. I don't want to push my kids into any profession unless they want it for their own lives. Loving what they do is more important to me than following in my footsteps. You came to my office, so do I assume that you have something to talk about?"

"Yes, Mr. Pierson. I received a call from our friend, Burt Snyder. You may remember that it was a tip from Burt that got the FBI to place the Hispanic women trafficking investigation back into active status again. Can we now be open about the information I received outside of business hours?"

"Of course, Liz. Even though we're not actively involved with any prosecution at this time, I have agreed to assist the FBI in any way that we can. Why don't you bring me up to date on what you know."

"Thank you, sir. It started with a meeting I attended with Burt, who introduced me as a retired sex crime investigator from Kentucky."

"I'd have loved to see the look on their faces to hear you described as 'retired.' How did Burt explain that?"

"He told them that I had moved to Erie with my fiancé because he got a job at the shipyard. But at that meeting, the need for someone to work undercover, to gain evidence, was discussed."

"Oh no!" Mr. Pierson said emphatically. I told you that you would never work undercover again. Your husband would skin me alive."

"I understand. No problem. Besides, my Spanish-speaking skills are sorely lacking. None of the hotel employees we met would be able to assist, for fear of losing their jobs. At this point, we don't know if any hotel managers are aware of what is happening, or possibly being paid to ignore it. Burt and I promised the hotel employees that their names would not be used. Most of the information they provided was very non-specific, other than making us aware that something was going on with a lot of women who didn't speak any English, and that some of them appeared to be physically abused."

"So, if we cannot use one of the employees undercover, what do we do?" Tom Pierson asked.

"Well, I didn't know this until Burt's call this morning, but he told me who initially roused his suspicions in this matter. A young, local Hispanic girl, who helped us with that yachter, Hendrickson, a couple years ago. She was the one who came to Burt with an incident that bothered her. She said she encountered three Hispanic women being manhandled by the men they were with at one of the larger hotels by the waterfront. None of the women seemed to speak English, and this local woman was able to speak with one of them in the restroom. She found out that none of them were there by choice, but their contractor for the hotel's cleaning labor services was pimping them out to hotel guests."

"I had wondered how old Burt had stumbled onto this. When he called to ask for an expert on trafficking, I told him what you did in your free time was unofficial. I'm so glad he called you. So, you still haven't mentioned the subject of someone undercover. I can't wait to hear."

"By now, maybe you might assume, the young lady that called Burt about that party, has agreed to work with the FBI on the case, but she has concerns about how the rescued women will be treated and how their cases will be handled. She told Burt that she would want to talk with someone at

INS to be sure the women will not just be deported without a proper hearing."

"After how well INS treated the children that you rescued a few years back, I think we can get INS on board with her concerns. But first, I think we need to see if the FBI wants an untrained person working undercover. They may want one of their own."

"I understand. But like you've told me in the past, as good as most cops are, they still just look like cops. That's why you like using Burt for some of your critical investigations. He looks as far away from being a cop as one can get."

Tom laughed, "That's for sure. Is he still driving all those beat-up old cars?"

"The last one I saw was a nice Lexus, which he bought from the Sheriff's auction. He left all the fender damage un-repaired after the drug dealer crashed during a chase. He said it runs great, but the visible damage lets him blend in during surveillance. And before you ask, he is still wearing that dirty, old raincoat he had two years ago."

Tom chuckled and shook his head. It was not so farfetched for Burt to be purposefully driving a damaged car around town.

"So, if the FBI agrees, Burt thinks this woman can work undercover? Any idea how and where that would be?" Tom asked Liz.

"I think that must be decided by the FBI if they agree. I'm sure we could get her into the hotel staff, but if there is a way to get her inside the contractor's organization, that would be the best. So, can you get this idea on the agenda for the meeting with the FBI? I told Burt to ask the young woman to be available, in case they want to meet with her."

"I'll call Sal Dominico right away to see what he thinks."

"Oh yes, I nearly forgot. Burt knows Agent Dominico from back in the days when Burt was with the FBI. They're still friends."

"Then I think I will include the fact that it was Burt who suggested this young woman. If Dominico knows Burt well, he'll know that this is something Burt has given a lot of thought to." "Thanks, Mr. Pierson. Let me know if I need to put Burt on alert, so he can have her attend."

Liz called Burt and told him about her meeting with Tom Pierson. If making Lucy go undercover as one of the hotel's staff was added to the agenda for the meeting the next day, Liz said she would call Burt again so he could plan to have Lucy and Burt attend the meeting.

Burt was pleased and immediately called Lucy who sounded a little unsure about the idea. Burt could hear the hesitation in her voice. "What's wrong, Lucy? I can hear it in your voice," he asked her.

"I'm not sure if I'm qualified to be doing this, Burt. I'm a little afraid for myself, but what if I screw up and put those girls in danger. I want to help them, but I was awake all night realizing that I may have their lives in my hands."

"I do understand, Lucy. That's why I like you. You really do care about others, not just about yourself. If the FBI asks to meet you, I think you should state that concern to them, the same way you just did to me. Trust me, Lucy. These men know that they have victim's lives, and those of innocent bystanders in their hands. These FBI Anti-Trafficking Agents also have a heart, though they tend to hide it most of the time. They will certainly understand your concerns. Let's see how they answer you. You just might be surprised."

"Okay, Burt. One step at a time. I'll agree to attend the meeting if they want to talk to me. But no promises about what my decision might be. When do you think they'd want me there? I'm working tomorrow, but I could ask for some time off in the afternoon."

"I'm sure it would be after lunch. If they agree to meet with you, I will ask them to delay your coming until mid-afternoon. Would that work?"

"That's fine. Thanks," Lucy answered.

"And by the way, Lucy. I told them about your deportation concerns, and my contact is working on that. She knows the INS people in Pittsburgh, and she agreed with your concern."

"Does this happen to be the same lady you were working with when we helped your surveillance of that yacht guy? I think she was a lawyer, but doing some undercover work at the time."

"Yes. I may have let the cat outa' the bag on that. I'm not sure if I was supposed to say anything about her involvement just yet."

"Well, I won't mention it. However, if I take on this investigation role, I may want to talk with her, seeing she has experience in this covert stuff. I'd like to hear about what she did, and pick her brain for advice before I agree."

"I think that would be a great idea. I think the two of you will really hit it off. I already told her that you very much remind me of when I first met her."

"I really look forward to getting to know her. Thanks, Burt."

10

PREPARING FOR VICTIMS

Liz knew she needed to consider how to handle the women rescued during the sting, based on her last trafficking sting operation experience. She had been able to find a local Rescue Center to handle the local girls who came from abusive homes, during that last sting. But when they found the Chinese, Moldovan, and Bulgarian children rescued during those same stings, they struggled to find people who could help and who also spoke their languages. Liz was worried that they were bound to be faced with the same problem this time around, and she wanted to prepare for that in advance.

Beth was one of the older teen girls who had stayed at the Rescue Center after being rescued. She was training to be a counselor and was now working on staff as a counselor-in-training at the rescue center. Beth's first-hand experience with being in an abusive home and having been lured into the world of trafficking meant that she easily gained the trust of the young women taken to the rescue center. They trusted her because she had experienced *"the life"* as the girls referred to it.

So, Liz asked Mr. Pierson if she could work on finding Spanish-speaking help, knowing that they would eventually need it, once the trafficking ring was broken.

Tom wondered if Lucy, the young lady who will be working undercover, couldn't possibly help them.

"She may be of some assistance, Tom, but we need someone, or possibly more than one, who can stay with these women and counsel them until they are either placed in a home or possibly deported back to their home countries. If nothing else, we want a Spanish-speaking advocate who can present their case, for those who are seeking asylum in the United States, in court. If Lucy helps with the undercover investigation, she won't have much time to help each of them one-on-one."

"I see your point, Liz. What do you plan on doing to find people to help?

"First, I'd like to call that local Rescue Center that assisted with the young kids during our sting of that modeling agency a couple years ago. One of the girls we rescued is working there, and she may have some ideas. I don't think she is fluent in Spanish, but she may know where we can find some people to assist."

"Good idea as a start, Liz. Yes, I think it's a good idea to plan, so if you can work that into your caseload, go ahead. Just keep me informed."

"Thanks, Tom. I won't let this interfere with my other work."

Later the following day, Liz called the Family Rescue Center and talked to the director.

"Is Beth still working with you at the center?" Liz asked the director after a few minutes of small talk.

"Oh, goodness, yes. I couldn't continue here without Beth. She has been great at her training and counseling studies, and I can honestly say that she is teaching me how to run the shelter. She so fully understands the situations that these women and children have experienced. We are all in awe of how well the families interact with Beth."

"Oh, I'm so happy that Beth has worked out so well. Knowing where she came from, I worried about how she was going to deal with life."

"Not only has Beth helped the families we take in at the center, but I truly believe that the work she does here has helped her deal with her demons. Helping others is her therapy."

"That's just wonderful to hear," Liz said.

"I have a feeling that checking on Beth was not the main reason for your call, Liz. What prompted your call?"

"Ahh, yes. I did get off track a little. But I'm so happy to hear about Beth's success. The reason I called, which may even involve Beth from what you've told me, is that I wanted to see if you have any Spanish-speaking help at the rescue center. We may need some people fluent in Spanish to help with some rescues. Any help there?"

"We do get a few Hispanic families who speak minimal, broken English. We've asked a few girls at the University to help translate for serious issues, like reading legal documents to the mothers. But otherwise, we've just muddled along.

Beth has picked up a little Spanish from talking with them, but she's certainly not fluent."

"Well, that sounds hopeful. Would you ask Beth if she knows any local Hispanic women who speak enough Spanish to help us? At this point, I don't know if it would be a few women or maybe even twenty. If we have a lot of rescues, how much room would you have to house them temporarily?"

"We've grown since you were here two years ago. We have twenty private rooms for families and two small dormitories: one larger one for women and a smaller one for the boys. The private rooms can accommodate six people comfortably. Except on occasion, we are seldom over 70% occupancy. So, I think we can help you for a limited stay time, at least."

"That sounds promising. I will be sure to ask for funding to help with your expenses. After you've consulted Beth, would you call me about the Spanish speaker situation?"

"Sure thing. Beth is working with a group of single moms right now. I'll talk with her once she finishes that class. Those young moms just love her."

"Thanks, I'll wait to hear from you," Liz said.

Two hours later, Liz was at her desk when her desk phone rang. It was Beth.

"Miss Liz, it was wonderful to hear that you had called our director. I have wanted to call you so many times but didn't want to disturb you. You don't know how grateful I am that you took such an interest in me, and helped me get back to a normal life."

"Beth, you've always had it in you to succeed. You just needed the opportunity to be surrounded by people who appreciated you for the right reasons and encouraged you to use your talent for working with people."

"Yes, I agree, Miss Liz. But many of the girls I see here at the Center have been handled by authorities who think that girls who sell their bodies are willing participants. They think that all those girls chose that life. The authorities don't understand that girls from abusive homes and those abused by a boyfriend or spouse, just don't know how to escape. But you, Miss Liz, seemed to know that we just needed a safe way to escape. Thank you so much!"

"Beth, I was lucky that my job in Law Enforcement allowed me to witness how young girls and boys were tricked into that life or were afraid for their lives if they refused to cooperate once they were abducted. If they didn't have a family to help them, they were trapped. I always tried to find a safe refuge for anyone who did not have a loving family to return to. For you, your dedication to those young kids we rescued two years ago, impressed your director so much that she wanted to continue with your training and education. But your dedication was the key! If it wasn't for your sincere desire to help others, you might have failed. I'm very proud of you, Beth."

"Well thank you again, Miss Liz. But I understand that you may soon need Spanish-speaking help. I have picked up some basic Spanish from working with the Hispanic kids in the families who stay at our shelter. But my boss said that you may need a little more fluency for translating documents and communicating with the rescued girls, is that right?"

"That's right, Beth. These women are from Central and South America, and some may need help with applying for asylum in the United States. But other than that, many of them have probably been sexually abused and they will need an understanding shoulder to cry on. Someone to give them hope. I remembered the young Moldovan girl who was so distraught when I brought her to the shelter, and even though you could not speak her language, she bonded with you."

"Oh, yes! I remember Linnea. Everyone thought her name was Olga, but that was her sister's name. Olga had died from repeated rapes, and they found her body buried in the garden. Linnea was so traumatized that she swayed like a caged animal. I could see the trauma in her eyes, and I believe she saw the same in me when she looked into my eyes. With that mutual understanding, she let me hold her and without speaking, we became sisters."

"If I asked you to do the same for these Hispanic women, would I be imposing on you, Beth? I don't want to make you revisit those demons you've left behind."

"That's not how it works, Miss Liz. I may never fully get rid of those demons, as you call them. But by showing my understanding for others who have lived through similar experiences, and showing my compassion, it continues to heal me as well. I love to see the terrible look in these abused girls' eyes melt away when we communicate. It doesn't require a lot of words. We sometimes just hold hands and cry together. They are looking for understanding, and I think I provide that for them."

"You're a wonderful person, Beth. I had a hard time dealing with what I saw regularly. I don't know how you do it, but I'm so glad that you *CAN* do what you're doing."

"That's because you only saw the problems. You have a loving relationship to go home to each day. That makes it harder to go back the next day, like you did."

"I now understand that. My husband helped me through the trauma I was experiencing with those young kids a couple years ago. He was a wonder! Until I accepted his help, I internalized too much of what I was seeing. Do you have someone you can talk to, so you don't try to handle all of this alone?"

"Funny you should ask, but I never thought I'd want to call another man a friend, after seeing the bad side of so many. But about three months ago, we had a young man come into the shelter. He had been abused for many years by a minister at his church, who was supposed to be the Youth Group leader. I saw the same look of distrust in his eyes as I was seeing in the eyes of the abused girls. Our Center's director asked me if I could help him, and I was very wary. I guess that I didn't trust men anymore. But Larry cried with me as we shared our pasts, and we have remained very close. I think we are just good friends, but I actually could picture our relationship becoming more serious. Larry is just as scared of that possibility as I am."

"I want you to be careful. But I'm also happy that you have found a possible personal relationship in your future. We all need someone to trust and hopefully to love in our life. We cannot deal with all the tough stuff alone."

"Yes, I'm beginning to see that. I can feel the relief in my heart when I share a bad day with Larry, and just like me, he says that it helps with his issues to talk to someone who has also experienced similar issues in their life. It had never occurred to me that men could experience abuse, even though I've seen the data that one out of every twelve kids trafficked are boys, Larry's abuse was right here, and his parents never noticed. But back to your current problem, Miss Liz. I will look for some serious, Spanish-speaking girls in my old neighborhood. I'll let you know if I find some who are willing to help."

"Thank you, Beth. Let's keep in touch. Maybe you and Larry could come to meet my husband, Steve. I'd love to meet him."

"I think we'd both enjoy a social outing. Larry and I have spent most of our time together here, at the Rescue Center. It's hard to forget our pasts in this place. I love my work here, but I'm starting to see that I need more personal time."

"Fantastic. You've come a long way over the last two years, young lady. I'm very proud of you and happy with what your future holds. We'll talk again soon."

11

LUCY'S MEETING

Burt picked Lucy up in his beat-up Lexus about a week after they met with Emma and Izzy. Liz had finally called to inform him that the FBI was very interested in speaking with Lucy. It turns out that Sal Dominicio had been impressed with Lucy's ability to pick up on what was going on and had assured Liz that Lucy would be well-trained before sending her undercover and that she would be well protected from harm.

"Would 3 o'clock work for me to get Lucy to the meeting?" Burt asked Liz. "She told her boss she needed to leave the store around 2:30, and I can pick her up and get her right over to the meeting place."

"I'm sure that'll be fine, Burt. These meetings tend to take a while when they have an active investigation to discuss. Sal said that they were very pleased with Lucy's willingness to assist them, and even more impressed by her concern over possible deportation. Tell Lucy not to hold back with her concerns, because the FBI has invited an INS agent to this meeting. I don't think that INS is officially involved right now, but Sal wanted them to hear Lucy's concerns."

"Thank God that Sal is involved. He may be a 'by-the-book' agent, but he has a conscience and a good heart."

Lucy walked out of the store where she worked and Burt was parked across the street and had the window down on his Lexus. He waved to Lucy and she jay-walked over to his car.

"I see you've had a little accident. Are you waiting to get it repaired?" Lucy asked as she settled into the passenger seat of Burt's car.

Burt chuckled. "Well, I've decided to leave the damaged fender. I don't like driving a car that stands out too much if I'm tailing someone. But don't worry, I've made all the important mechanical repairs."

For the first time, Lucy realized how unusual this guy Burt was. Here he was driving a damaged car and dressed in unusual clothing. Burt called it his 'street person' garb.

When Burt parked in the lone handicapped parking spot outside the courthouse, where the meeting was taking place, and placed a handicapped placard on his rearview mirror, Lucy audibly gasped.

"Technically, I am handicapped," Burt explained to Lucy. "I never use these parking spots unless I'm going to be late for an appointment."

Lucy was seeing a very different side of Burt today. She wondered if his handicap was physical or mental.

"Let's get into the office, Lucy. And remember, my FBI friend wants you to question them hard about your deportation concerns. There's going to be an INS agent at the meeting, but they'll be there in an unofficial capacity at this point. I think my friend was able to get INS to send someone. But unless the INS agent introduces himself as such, I think you should act as though INS is not in the room."

"I understand, Burt. But I'm really nervous about being here. I come from a very different class of people, and I grew up not trusting authority figures. I don't think they are going to like me."

"You know, Lucy, I think you should start out your comments with that exact statement. There may be some top agents in the FBI who think that way, but the men and women at this level, working as Field Agents, come from pretty normal backgrounds. I think you may be surprised by their reaction if you tell them that."

Again, Lucy looked at Burt like he was not being serious. She still felt nervous, but she decided she had nothing to lose, and she would follow Burt's advice.

Liz met them at the reception desk.

"We're going to use one of the larger conference rooms upstairs," she said, and she quickly led them back into the hallway and toward the elevator. Liz saw the fear in Lucy's eyes and responded by giving her a serious side hug.

"I know this may seem scary, but I've been in the meeting this afternoon, listening to these people. They are very worried that you may not like them. They need your help, and they want to impress you," Liz said to Lucy.

"They want to impress me?" Lucy said. "I'm a nobody and they are the trained cops. Why would they feel like they need to impress me?"

"Once you meet Mr. Dominico, I think you'll understand. He's about as normal as one can get. He not just needs you for this investigation, but he is so impressed that you recognized this problem, and want to help. Just act normally, Lucy. He will quickly put you at ease."

After making their way through several halls, Lucy, Liz, and Burt came to the room where everyone was waiting. Burt told Liz he would wait out in the hallway. The twelve people in the room stood up and smiled when they entered. Lucy was shocked to see such a large group. Three of them were women, but their pleasant smiles helped to calm her nerves.

A handsome man with graying hair came around the table and took Lucy's hand with both of his. "Miss Chavez, thank you so much for coming. I won't introduce all of the team just yet, but they will introduce themselves as they describe their roles in our investigation. But first, let me tell you how pleased we are that you agreed to meet with us. We've saved a seat at the table over here." Sal led Lucy to her seat.

As Lucy was seated, she turned to Sal and asked, "Can I say something first?"

"Of course, Miss Chavez. Whatever you'd like to say, we're all ears."

"Well, first, please call me Lucy." Sal nodded.

"On the drive over, I told Burt that I come from a part of society that grew up not trusting authority, whether it was at school or the cops. Sorry, I mean policemen. So, I'm not sure that I should be here," Lucy said, looking around the room and studying the faces that peered back at her.

"Several of the group chuckled a little, and one man got Sal's attention, saying, "Sal, can I start by answering Lucy?"

Sal said, "Lucy, this is Dominic Ruffalo. Dominic works in the Washington Office, and we asked him to be part of our team. Yes, Dominic, please respond to Lucy."

"Lucy, I know exactly how you feel. I grew up in Brooklyn, never met my father, and my mom worked several jobs to keep me and my sister fed and clothed. By age 9, I was part of a New York gang and was constantly in trouble. Luckily, I avoided jail time, but I was on a first-name basis with a young District Attorney, and the Juvenile Judge greeted me as Dom when I entered his courtroom because he saw me so often. This one time, I had been caught breaking windows in a factory warehouse, and the judge said, 'Dom, what are we going to do with you? You're too good to be throwing your life away like this.'"

Lucy said, "Wow, that sounds just like my brother. How did you go from court to the FBI?"

"It wasn't an overnight process, but that young Assistant District Attorney, a lady named Rosalie, asked the judge if she could refer me to a counselor whom she knew. She had discussed this with the judge before my appearance because the judge quickly said yes. The judge entered a judgment into the record that if I attended counseling sessions, the charges would be dropped, but if I appeared before him again, he would start treating me like a criminal."

"Wow. That was one cool judge," Lucy said.

"Yes, and Miss Rosalie, that DA, was not about to take it easy on me. She called my mother and asked my mom to take me to her office the next day. And my mom wasn't happy, because she had to miss work at the hospital. When we arrived at the DA's office, Miss Rosalie told my mom that they needed to get me away from those gang members, or I'd end up in jail. The look on my mother's face sent chills down my spine. Then she led us down the hall to another office that was labeled, Jorge Martinez, Juvenile Corrections Officer."

"Wow. That wasn't a counselor, that's a cop!" Lucy said.

"You bet!" Dominic said. "And I was really scared. And my mother began glaring at me again, which was even scarier. But Mr. Martinez turned out to be my savior. He started hard as nails, even telling my mom that I was headed down the wrong road. He made me come to the jail with him three days a week after school while he was meeting with young inmates. I now know that he really had to pull some strings to get a kid into the jail with him. And on Saturdays, when I normally hung out with those punks in that gang, Mr. Martinez made me volunteer at a local homeless shelter. I helped serve food, and the other volunteers even made me clean the toilets and pick up the garbage outside. Mr. Martinez worked me hard like that for three months. Then he got me on a neighborhood baseball team, a soccer team, and other activities. I was so busy that I had no time to get into trouble."

"That still doesn't explain how you got into the FBI," Lucy said.

"Jorge never let me go, entirely. Once I got into sports and stayed out of trouble, he called me to his office every few weeks. My grades in high school improved, and when I was nearing graduation, Jorge asked what I wanted to study in college. I had never even considered college. Most kids in my neighborhood never gave college a first thought, no less a second one. But Jorge said, 'I think you'd make a good cop. How about a Criminal Justice degree?'"

"That Martinez guy was something else. So, you went to college?"

"I did. And again, with Jorge's help, obtaining scholarships and State Aid. After college, Jorge found me a job in the Gang Enforcement Section, just down the hall from his office. That's when the FBI was looking for help in a new, anti-gang section, because of interstate drug trafficking. So, Lucy, that brings me to the here and now, and I don't want to hear you saying that you shouldn't be here. At least you're starting out with a sense of helping people you see in trouble. It took Mr. Martinez nearly a year to break through my hardened exterior. I look up to you and respect your being such a responsible, caring person."

"Thank you, Mr. Ruffalo, but I still feel a little intimidated by all these people." "If you are Lucy, then please call me Dom."

One of the women in the group then asked Sal if she could speak. "Of course, Theresa, please add what you'd like to say," Sal replied.

"Lucy, I'm Theresa Savage. I'm probably one of those girls you hated in school. I came from a good family and got good grades in high school. My parents sent me to a private college and with all of that, I was headed nowhere. I think my parents hoped I'd marry some rich attorney, have kids, and hang out at the County Club. I did okay in college but was drifting. Then I attended a career day sponsored by my college and the FBI had a table there. All of the other students were talking to the big companies, like consulting firms and research labs. There was nobody at the FBI's desk and I decided to sit and chat, with no real interest in joining the FBI. I wasn't interested in arresting drug traffickers or investigating the Mafia."

"I can understand that," Lucy said. "So, what happened?"

"When I sat down, rather than giving me a sales pitch, the young woman at the desk said, 'So, tell me what turns you on in life? And I don't mean drugs.' I was a bit shocked by her question, and her joking about drugs. It wasn't what I expected. Then the older gentleman at the desk said, 'People think that all the FBI does is chase kidnappers, bank robbers, and drug runners, but we may have areas that might interest you.'"

"That would have surprised me too," Lucy said. "So, what did you tell them?"

"I had been volunteering at a daycare for single moms at my college, so I told him I liked working with kids. The guy said, 'I know just what job you'd be perfect for. Would you like to hear more?' I was intrigued, so I told him to continue."

"I don't think the FBI was running a daycare, so what job did he describe?" Lucy asked, with a smirk on her face.

"Well, it was a lot of training, but I went into cyber-intelligence, looking for people on social media, luring kids into potentially abusive situations. At first, I thought it was just teenagers who were being contacted by abusers, but with kids today having cell phones at such young ages, I've found kids as young as seven years old answering requests to meet at a local mall, purportedly to play games together. I still do that kind of work, but because of you, and the young women who are in trouble here, I was asked to assist you. As a plus, I also speak pretty good Spanish, which was my minor in college. So, if you agree to help us, I'm your right-hand-girl, if you want me to be."

Lucy was impressed by what she was hearing. As the meeting progressed, she heard from them all. A few of them turned out to be the 'cop types', and she may not have been impressed by them at first, but each one had a specific job that fit into their plan, from wire-tapping the contractor's communications, surveillance, and even some tough guys who could rescue the girls, or even rescue her if things turned bad.

Sal Dominico told Lucy that she would spend as much time as she had available with Theresa Savage, learning what to say, what not to say, and how to get the information they would need to prosecute the traffickers.

Lucy asked Theresa, "How much time do you think it will take to prepare me, Theresa?"

"That depends," Theresa replied. "Do you live alone? If so, do you have a sofa where I can sleep? I know you have a job, which for now, you can't get away from. But if I can spend your non-working hours talking with you about how you will need to act, I think we can have you ready in just a few days. Then, once we get you inside their organization, I understand you will be able to take some vacation time, while you work with us. I will act as your roommate and be with you as much as possible."

"I will probably have a lot more questions, Theresa, but you are welcome to use my sofa. I've missed having a roommate, so this may be a good change. But now I need to ask a tough question. I'm Hispanic, third generation. But I have some ancestors who probably were illegals. I understand that we want to keep out the terrorists and criminals, but these girls are victims, not bad people. If they want to go back home, that's fine, but their culture will ostracize them once their countrymen find out that they have been used for repeated sex. They will need help, so if we are automatically going to deport them, I don't want to be part of it."

Sal looked around the room, he didn't know what to say. Finally, the middle-aged woman sitting quietly in the back of the room smiled at Sal and said, "Okay, Sal. I've heard enough and I'm impressed by Miss Chavez. Can I answer her?"

"Please, Mattie. I was hoping you'd volunteer. Thank you," Sal said.

"Lucy, my name is Mathilda Mathews. I prefer Mattie, so please forget Mathilda. Only my mother calls me that. I am here unofficially at this point, but I'm with the Pittsburgh Office of INS. I don't think I need to explain INS, right?"

"I'm aware of INS, Mattie. That's why I asked the question."

"So, then Lucy, my boss asked me to sit in on this meeting and report the situation to him. From what I understand, we may have from twenty to fifty, possibly more young women who were lured by this trafficker to work in the United States with the promise of becoming U.S. citizens. They now find themselves working basically as indentured slaves, and also being used for sex. And you've witnessed some of the women being used in this situation?"

"Yes, I attended a party and saw three young girls being pawed over by the men they were with., None of the girls could speak English, and they were very fearful. I got to speak with one of the women in the restroom, and she verified my suspicions."

"Then Lucy, let me tell you what I will recommend to my boss in Pittsburgh. After we interview the women who are rescued, we will investigate their backgrounds with the counties from which they came. If they have no serious criminal history, and if they are afraid to go back to their country, they can apply for asylum in the United States. Personally, as a concerned female myself, I want to help them. However, we can probably grant their asylum request, but we cannot counsel them."

"That was going to be my next question," Lucy said. "I don't want them to be just dumped out on the streets of Erie. They are far away from their homes and don't understand how to survive here, and how to support themselves. What happens to them?"

That's when Liz spoke up. She had remained quiet up until now. "Agent Dominico, can I jump in on that concern?"

"Thanks, Liz. And please, it's just Sal. I know that you've been working on that aspect already."

"Thanks, Sal. And Lucy, this was my greatest concern ever since we heard about this situation from Burt. Erie has had experience with foreign nationals being rescued and needing help. We had both Chinese and Eastern European youths rescued, far away from home, and unable to return safely. We were able to locate homes for them to stay in, the younger ones even being adopted. A young Moldovan boy we rescued, was fostered by one of the counselors who works downstairs in this building. He's about to graduate high school next year. I've also been in touch with our local family rescue center. They are looking for local Spanish-speaking volunteers to help with translation, and the center said they can house and feed these women short term until we locate permanent homes. We've even found a means for the women to be employed, working for a janitorial service. This janitorial owner speaks Spanish, and he only uses legal workers. He'd love to have more help."

"Wow, Liz. I never expected that you'd have put all this together."

"I need to give my husband some credit," Liz said. "He recommended the janitorial company because they clean his office at work."

"Just one more question," Lucy said. "When do we start? I want those girls out of there." Everyone nodded and smiled.

12

THE ROOMMATE

The meeting slowly evolved into some small groups as they stood around the room. Liz and Lucy seemed to be tossed from one group to the next, answering questions that each group was discussing. The IT people wanted to ask how and where Lucy was comfortable wearing a wire. They liked her full head of hair, which could easily hide a mini microphone/transmitter. Mattie wanted to hear more about the rescue center and the local Spanish speakers. Sal and Dom wanted to reassure Lucy that they would have agents close by to come to her rescue if they heard anything threatening. Theresa assured Lucy that she could coach her on what questions to ask. The questions could not raise suspicion, but would slowly incriminate the contractor.

Sal told Lucy that they had already researched the contractor and knew their local personnel. They planned to arrest one of their office workers, a woman with a criminal record, and submit a properly prepared resume' for Lucy to replace that woman in their office. Lucy was impressed by all the work they had done in such a short time.

When the meeting finally dissipated, Theresa Savage approached Lucy and asked her when a convenient time for her would be to start being Lucy's right-hand girl. "Seriously," Lucy said, "I was hoping you could come home with me and help make dinner."

"That would be wonderful," Theresa responded. "The sooner we start talking, the more comfortable you will become with the situation. I like your style, young lady!"

Burt, who hadn't attended the meeting, was waiting for Lucy when she walked out into the courtroom lobby.

"Burt, meet my new roommate, Theresa. Can you please drive us home?"

"I think that means that you were satisfied with their answers," Burt said.

"And we like what Lucy Chavez is made of!" Theresa answered before Lucy could respond. "Thanks, Theresa," Lucy said, with a big smile on her face.

Burt stopped by Teresa's hotel to pick up her luggage, and then dropped Lucy and Teresa at Lucy's apartment. After chatting over dinner, Theresa wasted no time coaching Lucy on what to say and how to say it to lead the other office personnel in the contractor's office to start speaking and revealing where the workers were from and what they were being used for. Even if it wasn't revealed that the girls were

being used as sex-for-sale, Lucy could still get them to reveal where the girls were being housed, how they were being transported to and from work, and which hotels were paying for their labor services.

Later, Lucy could try to find out the names of those in the hotels' management personnel who were involved. Lucy was to act naïve, speaking English, but with some 'Spanglish' thrown in, to make the others think she wouldn't notice, or even care when they talked more freely about what was going on. Theresa said that after a few days inside, they would rig Lucy with a wire, just in case she was searched on the first few days there.

All of this left Lucy worried. However, Theresa was a good teacher, and within a couple of days, they started practicing some conversations that Lucy could start with her fellow workers. This helped Lucy's level of confidence.

On their second day together, Lucy asked Teresa to tell her more about her normal FBI job, fighting the cyber-attacks on young kids. It seemed like a very unusual, yet serious job.

Teresa said, "Well let me tell you a real-life story, which is typical of what we do. A young boy in a Western suburb of Chicago, just 13-years-old, was texting with a girl he had originally met in an on-line chat program. The girl said she was from California and she sent him some pictures to keep him interested. Once she located where he lived, she said she was going to visit her aunt in Chicago, and maybe they could finally meet."

"Oh my! I see where this is headed," Lucy said.

"Of course, our life experience throws up red flags, but for a young boy, starting to experience those raging hormones, he wanted to meet her. They planned to meet in a parking lot near the boy's home."

"Didn't the boy's parents warn him?" Liz asked.

"His mother was a single mom, but she did notice her son's cell phone 'tinging' all the time, so she looked at some of the messages one day while her son was taking his shower. Luckily, she had a friend who was a dispatcher for the local police department, and she asked her for advice. The dispatcher mentioned the situation to the Chief, and the Chief called the local FBI Field Office. I was sent to assist the Chicago office, and we placed the young boy under surveillance, just in time. The very next day, he went to the place the girl told him they'd meet, and when he arrived, two women grabbed him and pulled him into their car. Our two unmarked cars pulled up, one in front and one behind the car, and we rescued the boy."

"That must have really traumatized the boy," Lucy said.

"Yes. If we'd have had more warning, we would have tried to avoid using the boy himself as bait, thus avoiding that trauma. But we had no time to communicate with the cyberattacker like we would when warned of these situations earlier in the process. Then we can take control of the situation and lure the traffickers into our own trap, instead of coming to a last-minute rescue like this one."

"And it was two women who were going to kidnap him?" Lucy said in surprise.

"It usually is women, even older teen girls, who abduct kids, because it creates a sense of trust. Kids might be warned to be wary of some guy in a situation like that, but their minds don't seem to be suspicious of a young woman asking them to get into their car. Girls will befriend another young, pretty girl on the beach, chatting about clothes or boyfriends. When the older girl invites them to come to her car for a cold bottle of water, they never suspect that the water has been drugged. The next thing they know, they have been driven three states away and are the next victim of sex-trafficking."

"Wow!" Lucy reacted. "What a job you have!"

"It has it's tough days, but also very rewarding," Teresa said.

Two days later, Sal called to find out what Lucy knew about timekeeping. He said he had scheduled an appointment for Lucy to be interviewed at Trainor Labor Company in two days. The company had lost their timekeeper, she being the one who had been arrested, and they were looking for a replacement.

"Oh my! I'm not sure if I know anything more than filling out my own timecard," Lucy said.

"That's a start," Sal laughed. "Tomorrow, we'd like you to take that leave of absence from your job. We've found a career timekeeper who said he can give you enough information to satisfy them. I think you may not need to be inside their operation for more than two weeks to get some good intel. Then, we will have you mess up something in the timekeeping so that they fire you. That will be a good way to have a clean break, and not get them suspicious about why you were there."

"So, you think we can get enough information on them in just two weeks?" Lucy asked.

"The important intel will be to find out where the women are housed and how they are being transported. Our sting will be to rescue all of the women at once, to be sure that none of them are harmed or moved once we make our raid on the operation. Once we have them safe, our translators will get their statements, which can be used in evidence against the traffickers."

"I'm happy that you're doing this in a way to prevent any of the girls being harmed, Sal." "I promised in our meeting that we would protect the victims, Lucy, and I meant it." "Well thanks for taking that point seriously, Sal."

"I told you we had a serious team. So, please trust us. We all have families, and we really feel compassion for innocent victims."

"I guess my impression of cops was tainted by where I grew up. I didn't intend to insult you, Sal."

"I understand that, Lucy. You typically saw the side of law enforcement that deals with the bad guys. My guys may not treat the perps with kid gloves either. But the concern you have for these girls is shared by all of us. They aren't the bad guys."

"Okay. Now I think I understand. I just don't want these girls sent back to the hell they may have had back home. But then, I also wanted to kick every one of those guys in the balls that were manhandling those girls that night. I only got to land one on my date, once I found out what was happening."

"I like your style," Sal said. "You didn't just ignore the problem and run away. You went to Burt in order to help those girls. I have nothing but respect for you, Lucy."

Lucy's boss wished that she had given more notice before putting in her request for a leave of absence. However, because Lucy was her top sales person, and she had promised her some time off, she agreed to the last-minute request.

Lucy spent a quick day with the timekeeper that the FBI had found to train her, and Lucy was surprised by how much she understood. The trainer gave her several key points to stress during her interview and said that she should call him from work if she ran into anything that seemed confusing.

The following morning, Lucy took an Uber ride to the Trainor Labor Company's office, which was in a small building in a partially abandoned industrial complex. Obviously, they were not trying to impress their clients with anything fancy. The office had a keypad security door and two small windows overlooking the parking lot.

Lucy rang the buzzer next to the door and was met by an overweight, scruffy-looking man wearing a polo shirt that was a size too small for him. Lucy wondered why she had bothered to dress up for the interview.

"Hi, I'm Lucy Chavez," Lucy said, introducing herself. "I'm here to interview for the timekeeper's job."

"Wow. Nice!" the man answered. "You'd sure be an improvement," he added, with a leering look that Lucy did not appreciate.

Lucy did not respond to the man's advances. Instead, she silently followed him inside. Once inside and seated, Lucy asked the man, "What would you like to know about my experience?"

"Well, I saw your Resume' and the boss said it looked great. I just want to be sure though, can you speak Spanish? We have a lot of Spanish-speaking employees."

"I grew up in a Spanish-speaking home, so Spanish is my first language," Lucy said. "But I have twelve years of English-speaking schooling, plus I'm studying for an Associate Degree in Business Administration. That's why I started doing time-keeping. May I ask you your name?"

"Oh, sorry. You can call me Trev. It's short for Trevor. Trevor Hobson. I handle personnel issues for our clients."

"Okay, Trev. Who are Trainor's clients? Tell me a little about Trainor Labor, and who I would be doing timekeeping for. How many employees does Trainor have?"

Lucy wondered if her questions might cause Trevor to be suspicious, but he seemed to expect such questions from a prospective employee, so, he answered, "Most of our clients are the local hotels, but we also have some hotels and casinos over in New York state. We have about sixty employees locally, but you will be handling the time for about 120 total, including those in New York and a few around Cleveland."

"So, I'm handling the time to pay the employees?" Lucy asked.

"That gets handled by another office," Trevor said. "Your main job is to prepare invoices for the hotels and casinos, based upon the timecards that you will receive."

"Okay, I understand," Lucy said. "I will prepare the invoices and mail them to the clients."

"To expedite payment, we have the invoices hand-delivered in most cases. Our managers deliver most of them in New York and Ohio, but we may ask you to deliver some of them locally. Do you have access to a car if we need you to do that?"

"I have a friend that lets me use his car. If you let me know when you need me to have a car available, that won't be a problem," Lucy said.

"Well then, I showed your resume' to the boss and he had you checked out at that local college you attended. He said that if I was happy, and if you had good Spanish skills, you could start tomorrow. Will that work for you?" Trevor asked.

"That would be great," Lucy said. "I was just doing some part-time retail sales until I landed a timekeeping job. I notified my sales manager that if you hired me, I would be quitting that job. We haven't discussed pay yet, so that is my only other question, I guess."

"How does $1000 per week sound? Once you show us that you can handle it, we can bump it up a little. We don't have any benefits, so we pay a little better, knowing you need to cover your own health care and so forth. And if we ask you to deliver those invoices, we'll also cover your expenses as well."

"That sounds fair," Lucy said. "I have a friend who works at the locomotive factory as a timekeeper, and he said I could call him if I had questions."

"That's okay, but we expect you to keep our employee's names and our client's information confidential."

"Of course," Lucy said. "That was stressed in all of my Business Admin classes. You can trust me."

"I think you have the job then, Miss Chavez. I'll see you tomorrow morning at eight. We're a little behind in invoicing because our last girl left unexpectedly. So, you'll have to hit the ground running, as they say."

"I'm looking forward to it," Lucy said. "I'm well prepared and willing to work hard."

Lucy walked out and thought she would never take a real job working for someone like Trevor. The way he looked at her gave her the creeps. She wondered just how far up the ladder Trevor was in this organization.

13

THE DEBRIEF

After the interview, Lucy called for an Uber and returned to her apartment, where Theresa was waiting anxiously to hear how things went.

"What happened?" Theresa asked, sounding out of breath with apprehension.

"I was expecting a bunch of questions to test my knowledge of timekeeping," Lucy said. "But it sounded like that person you warned about getting a call, over at the University, did a great job telling them about my qualifications, so they just accepted that I could do the job. The guy stressed my being confidential about their employee and client info, but otherwise, he just hired me once I assured him that I could speak Spanish. He never said anything about my need to work with the Spanish-speaking employees, but I assume that will happen, seeing it was so important to him."

"That sounds good, Lucy. If they use you as an interpreter, you will be able to ask important questions."

"And another thing that came up, which may be important. They hand-deliver their invoices, and he mentioned that he may want me to do some of the local deliveries to their clients. He mentioned that the managers of the company deliver the invoices in New York state and some around Cleveland. He also said they have about sixty employees locally, and 120 in total."

"Wow! This guy opened up to you much more than I expected he would since it was the first time he met you. This is all great information. I guess we expected that they were supplying labor around Niagara Falls, but now you have pretty well confirmed it."

"I'm going to need a car for those deliveries on the days they ask me to deliver them. I told them that I could borrow a car from a friend. How will we handle that?" Lucy asked.

"Well, we can't have you showing up with a new car. Any ideas?" Theresa asked.

"I wondered if my friend, Burt, could let me borrow one of his beaters," Lucy said with a chuckle. "He buys old junkers to blend in, during his undercover work."

"That might be perfect," Theresa said. "The Agency could contract with him to use one of them. I'll have Sal talk to Burt. Knowing he respects you, I bet he'll agree."

"And one more thing," Lucy said. "This Trevor guy is a real scum bag. He kept eyeing me up like I was a hunk of meat. I'll bet he's using some of those girls himself. What a loser!"

Theresa relayed all of this information to Sal, while Lucy listened in. Sal told Theresa to compliment Lucy on a great first contact and asked that Lucy call him at any time if anything appeared to be going wrong.

14

THE JOB

The next morning, Lucy took an Uber to work. Trevor was there to meet her.

"My friend is okay with loaning me his car, and in fact, he now has a second car, so he is going to let me use one full time, rather than me taking an Uber to work every day. He's loaning me a real beater, but he says it runs fine."

"Ahh, that's great," Trevor said. "I won't have you making deliveries this week, because we need to catch up on the invoicing. But I may need you to do some deliveries next week. Thank your friend for loaning you the car. As long as it runs well, the looks don't matter. Is this a romantic friend? He must have some serious interest in you!"

"Well, let's just say he looks after my safety, but nothing romantic." Lucy hung her handbag on the chair where she would be working and turned to face Trevor.

"Okay, Trev. Show me what I need to do first," she said, rubbing her hands together expectantly. Lucy could tell that Trevor was trying to hit on her, he had even dressed a little better than he had the day before. That is to say, he was wearing a shirt that fit well enough to cover his belly. Trevor seemed to get the hint and changed the subject.

"Right. Here are the timecards for the employees." He reached out under the only other desk in the dingy small room and lifted a box filled with envelopes. "They're in separate envelopes for each client," he continued. "The client's name is on the outside of the envelope. On some of the employees' cards, you will see a red-X on some dates that they worked. We invoice those hours separately, at a higher rate. For now, just get the invoices done for the time without the red-X's. I'll handle those other times myself until you learn how things are done."

Lucy nodded, trying to follow along as Trevor continued to show her the ropes.

"The billing rate to the clients is $14.75 per hour. You can just add the normal hours together and the invoice will read, 'XXX employees for the week ending XXXX, with XXX total hours @ $14.75 per hour, for a total of $XXXX.' Do you understand?"

"That's pretty simple, Trev. But if you are only invoicing at $14.75 per hour, the employees aren't making much."

"They get compensated well. We supply a place for them to stay and all their meals. And those who work for those red-Xs get extra incentives. That's all you need to know for now."

"Sure thing, Trev. Do you have a list of the clients' contact information and addresses? I'll need those in order to address the invoices."

"Sure. There's a rolodex on your desk. It has the client names. You don't need to address it to anyone's attention.

The delivery person will know who to get the invoices delivered to."

Even without any real experience in such matters, Lucy was starting to see that this operation was keeping the names of those involved hidden. It was going to be tough getting details about the hotel management people who were involved. If this was a normal business relationship, the contact names would be part of the invoices. And only billing $14.75 per hour! No wonder the hotels wanted to

use these services. Lucy had an aunt who cleaned in office buildings, and she was earning $16.00 an hour, so obviously, Trainor Labor wasn't using anyone other than the trafficked people she suspected.

"So, Lucy," Trevor said, "we have twelve very important invoices to get done today. We want those invoices delivered tomorrow by Rob, one of our runners. I'd like you to accompany Rob on those deliveries so you would be able to make the deliveries for me in the future. Here are the twelve envelopes with timecards. You'll see the client's name on the front and you have the Rolodex on your desk with the clients' addresses. Put together one invoice for me to look over and I will see if you have the idea. Come over to my office when you have that first one done."

Lucy decided to start with the envelope that had the most timecards, which had Fiesta Bay Hotel written on the front. The timecards each had Trainor Labor Company printed across the top and a person's name was hand written beneath it. Most had first names only, and most of the names were Hispanic. However, two names popped out from the rest: Yellowbird and Kishi. Lucy had several Native Americans in her high school class, and one of them was named Kishi. She remembered asking the girl about her name, and she had been proud of its meaning: Night. Lucy saw that not only Hispanic girls were being used, but Indigenous girls as well. She assumed the Yellowbird name may have been either a Native American last name or a nickname that the girl used.

Then there were columns on the card for the date, hours worked, and some abbreviations that Lucy assumed were used to describe the work done on that day. Kishi had one of those Red-X notations one day, and so did another girl, called Marcella. Both girls had worked on the same day, so Lucy assumed they had been sent to party with men at the hotel on that day.

After Lucy prepared that first invoice, she printed it and went to Trevor's office for further instructions. She had kept it simple, addressed to the Fiesta Bay Hotel, stating the invoice was for the services of seventeen employees for the week of 12-18 July. The next line stated that a total of 884 hours had been worked at $14.75 per hour, and the following line read, Invoice Total: $13,039.00. Lucy asked, "Should I list the employee names on the invoice or the work they performed?"

"No, the clients have learned to trust us, as long as the work is done well. Print this on our letterhead, which you'll find in one of those desk drawers. When you finish the twelve invoices, bring them all to me. Just be sure to shred this sample and any mistakes you might make."

"Okay, Trev. I'll get back to work." Lucy believed that there might be cameras in the office, so on the way back to her desk, she stopped in the restroom. After making sure there were no hidden cameras in there, Lucy snapped a photo of the rough invoice as well as the three timecards she had hidden in her bra. The timecards belonged to Kishi, Yellowbird, and Marcella. She knew she had taken a chance hiding those timecards, but she felt they were important. She had dropped a stack of cards on the floor before leaving her desk and leaned over to pick them up. She had placed those three cards on top of the pile, so while gathering the cards under her desk, she slipped those three into her bra. In case she was being observed, she hoped that picking up and placing the other cards back on her deck would cover her deception.

When Lucy was done getting what she needed to get, she exited the restroom. Trevor was standing right outside the door when she opened it. The look in his eyes unnerved Lucy.

"Did I hear some camera snaps coming from inside the bathroom," he asked, looking suspiciously at Lucy.

Lucy had to think quickly. "Yeah, I was just taking a few selfies for my gram. I'm so proud to finally be working an office job, I thought I'd share a quick post with my followers after work. I hope that's okay."

Trevor seemed to relax as he eyed the draft invoice and cell phone in Lucy's hand, offering to show Trevor her selfies. "You young ladies and Instagram! It's okay to mention your new job here, yes, but that's all you can share. Remember, we respect the confidentiality of our clients and employees, so you cannot post anything that mentions them or even gives a hint of who they are. The same goes for our employees."

Lucy nodded and scurried off to her desk where she shredded the rough invoice and replaced the timecards in the envelope.

By noon, she had finished the twelve invoices. She was sure not to rouse Trevor's suspicions the rest of the day, even as she continued to make several trips to the restroom to photograph the timecards. She silenced the photo-clicking sound on her phone and was a little more discreet.

15

THE NEXT DEBRIEF

"**S**low down Lucy. I want to record all of this so we can report everything to Sal. We may forget some of it if we try to repeat it all later," Theresa said, asking Lucy to slow down as she went on non-stop as soon as she walked in the door later that evening.

So, Lucy poured them each a glass of her favorite Malbec and started to relay everything she had learned that day. Theresa listened intently and only interrupted a few times for clarification. Lastly, Lucy showed Theresa the photos she had taken of the sample invoice and the various timecards she had photographed throughout the day.

"Oh my, don't let them see that you are taking photos, Lucy."

"Unless they have cameras located in the bathroom stalls, they won't see me taking photos," Lucy said, giggling. "Although, Trevor did become a little suspicious the first time I took the photos. He was standing outside the bathroom door when I came out and it looked like he heard the sound of the camera clicking. I forgot to silence my camera sounds. But I had taken the selfies last, as you suggested, and I offered to show them to him."

Theresa covered her mouth with the palm of her hand. "You need to be very careful, Lucy. People like Trevor, people running illegal operations, are always highly suspicious. I would hope that they do not have cameras in the restrooms, but we don't know how paranoid these guys might be," Theresa said.

"There may be some smart guys in the organization, but Trevor isn't one of them. He only seems to be concerned with hitting on me every chance he gets. I think I can get a lot more details out of him just by letting him think I'm interested in him."

"Geez, Lucy! Don't let yourself get lured into something that will get you hurt. We need your help, but not like that."

"I know how to flirt without getting over-involved. Don't worry about me."

"Please be careful, Lucy. I don't want you hurt."

Lucy assured Theresa she'd be a little more careful, before adding, "Before I forget, I have the twelve clients' hotel names memorized. Let me recite them to you before I forget. It was pretty easy because I have been at the hotel bars at most of them." Lucy recited the list into Theresa's tape and then they called Sal to update him on what Lucy had learned.

After playing the tape for Sal, Lucy said, "By the way, Trevor is sending me out on the invoice delivery tomorrow with a guy named Rob. Trevor wants me trained so I can do them alone next time. So, I'll maybe meet some of the hotel staff that are involved. I may be able to get some information out of Rob while we're driving. How would you like me to handle that?"

Sal and Theresa both gave Lucy some ways to lead the conversation into areas that would be important for the investigation, But Sal ended by saying, "But Lucy, I don't want you acting too curious to raise suspicion. I would feel terrible if you were hurt during this operation."

"I know how to handle guys, Sal. Don't worry."

16

HOTEL DELIVERIES

The following morning, Trevor called Lucy into his office. There was a young man already there.

"Rob, this is Lucy. I want you to take her along on your deliveries today. She is our new timekeeper, and she prepared these invoices that you're delivering today. I want her to meet the people at the hotels in case we need her to make deliveries in the future. Understand?"

Rob sort of grunted his understanding with a guttural "Uh huh," but showed little interest in Trevor. Lucy worried that Rob was not happy with showing her his job.

"Are you ready to go, Lucy? Those twelve stops will take quite a bit of the day, so you two had better head out," Trevor said.

"Just a quick stop at the restroom and I'm ready, Trev. I'll meet you out front, Rob." Rob did not respond.

What's his deal, Lucy thought on her way to the bathroom. *If Rob wasn't happy about her tagging along, was he going to engage her in any sort of conversation?* She was worried about how the day was going to turn out.

Rob was waiting for her outside when Lucy was ready. He opened the passenger door for her when she came out. Lucy had not expected that. So, when Rob got into the driver's seat, she jumped right into it. "I hope you don't mind dragging me around town, Rob. I have no idea what goes on here, so I'll appreciate anything you can help me with."

"You sure you don't know what happens here?" Rob asked, a little sarcastically. "Not really," Lucy responded, sensing Rob's hostility waver just a little bit.

"Do you know anything about these workers?" Rob asked Lucy.

"I just started on Tuesday and prepared these invoices. I was surprised by how little the girls get paid, but that's about all I know."

"Paid? They don't pay them anything. They get to sleep in some dirty barracks behind an old, abandoned factory, and I've seen the crap they feed them because I deliver the food there. Unless they eat the leftovers on the trays left in the hotel rooms, they'd probably starve."

"Oh, my! What did I get myself into?" Lucy said. But now she also realized she had an ally and a good source of information. "So, this is some sort of illegal operation, is what you're saying?"

"It has to be," Rob responded. "I don't speak Spanish, but from what I can tell, all of the girls are Hispanic, and they all act scared around me, or any of the Anglos. I think this company has found a way to import people from Mexico or other Spanish-speaking countries. Several older ladies work at the barracks, and some of them are not treating the girls well. A couple of them are okay, and I've talked with them about the situation. They're afraid to speak up for fear of what the big bosses might do to them."

"I understand, Rob. But don't let on to Trevor or the people at the hotels that you know all of this. You can't help the girls if you get fired from this job. Tell me what you know about the people we meet today, and maybe we can find a way to help the girls. I'm shocked about all of this." "You really didn't know about any of this? You'll try to help them?" Rob said.

Lucy could hear the honest concern in Rob's voice, and responded, "Yes, I want to help the girls. I had no idea about the conditions you've just described."

For the rest of the day, Rob would tell Lucy about each hotel situation that he could. He described the persons they met, their attitude toward the working girls, and whether or not he thought they knew about the slave labor aspect of the situation. Some people he described as being part of the situation, not caring if the girls were not paid, and possibly being bribed by Trainor Labor. Others Rob described as too naïve to see what was happening, but at least were not in 'on the take.'

Lucy kept good mental notes but didn't want to raise Rob's suspicions by keeping written notes. She knew she would have a lot of new information to discuss with Theresa and Sal that evening.

Lucy arrived home to find Sal Dominico waiting inside her apartment's lobby.

"I didn't want to be presumptuous and go upstairs," Sal said, responding to Lucy's questioning look. I called Theresa to tell her I was coming over but told her I'd wait down here until you arrived. We also can't be sure that Trainor isn't watching your apartment, so I didn't want to arrive after you came home. If you don't mind, I bought some seafood and pasta for dinner. I'm an amateur cook, and I'll do my thing while you tell us about your day."

"Fantastic! Both your dinner plans and that you are here to discuss what I learned today. I was waiting to tell Theresa that we may need to call you about this great new info I've got. What a day! I can't wait to get this all recorded."

"Then lead the way, Lucy. I hope you like Frutti Di Mari! My wife thinks mine is better than any restaurant's version she's ever had."

"I'm up for that, and I'm hungry. Let's head upstairs."

Upstairs, at Lucy's apartment, Sal greeted Theresa and Lucy hugged Theresa. Their friendship was blossoming fast. "Wait until you hear this new development I have," Lucy started. "I was dreading this day, having to spend it with this guy Rob, who I'd not met, and assumed he would be another Trevor. Instead, Rob knows what's going on with the girls, though I'm not sure if he knows about some being used for the sex trade. He knows that they are being imported illegally and that they're not being paid. To put his position bluntly, 'he's pissed off' at the company for what they are doing. The problem is that his attitude toward Trevor this morning sorta' exposed his position, so I asked him to hide that attitude from them if he wanted to be able to help the girls. I told him if he got fired, it wouldn't help them."

"You didn't let on that you were here to help them, did you?" Sal asked.

"Oh no. I tried to act as surprised as possible by anything he shared throughout the day. I think that Rob believes that I am concerned about what he told me, but I don't think he suspects me at all. At first, I thought Rob could have been testing me, under directions from Trevor, but after you hear what else he shared over the day, I think we can be sure that Rob will be our ally in all of this. If nothing else, he will be a better witness to the inside workings of the operation than I would be."

"That's great news, Lucy. Where shall we start?"

"First of all, get me that list of the hotel clients for whom I prepared those invoices. The hotel names will jog my memory with the details we encountered throughout the day. Why don't we sit at the countertop by the kitchen, so that Sal can talk while preparing dinner? I told him that I was starving."

"Good idea," Theresa said. "I'll set up the digital recorder between us so we can save every bit of info that you can remember."

"Yes. I wanted so badly to make notes, but in case I was reading Rob wrong, I didn't want him to get suspicious. However, seeing Trevor wants me to start making these deliveries, I asked Rob at the end of the day to make me a list of the contact names at each hotel we visited, to help me with those deliveries in the future. He agreed to do that."

Sal then asked, "Are you at all worried about Rob's status with Trainor? I mean, if they intend to have you make these deliveries in the future, what will Rob be doing? I'm wondering if they've noted Rob's attitude and they plan to get rid of him. And I don't just mean firing him. What I'm hearing you say, makes me wonder about his safety. People like this are willing to kill someone they think is a threat. That's why we want to get your part of this operation done quickly, to get you out of harm's way before we take them down."

"Wow! I hadn't thought about that, Sal. I thought that Rob might just quit, but with all he seems to know, I'm worried that you could be right. Can we protect him somehow?" Lucy asked.

"I think the best way to do that is to convince Trevor that you need Rob's help for at least one more delivery run. Then we can get Rob out of there, basically taking him into protective custody. We'll make it look like he just ran away. From what you're saying, he may be a very good and willing witness."

"I like that plan," Lucy said. "So, let's start on the list of hotels. I asked Rob to start at the Fiesta Bay Hotel because that is where Kishi and Yellowbird work. I was curious about why the two Native girls worked there. Rob used the service entrance at all of the hotels. We never went to the main, corporate offices, but instead, we delivered the invoices to the Housekeeping Managers, or in a few cases, it was the Building Maintenance Manager. I was glad that we didn't enter the front doors, because I might have been recognized at some of the waterfront hotels, where I've frequented their restaurants."

"So, from what you saw today, upper management is trying to keep their distance from these contracts. Is that right?" Sal asked.

"At first, that's what I believed. And I think there is a mix of situations where upper management is not aware that this is going on, or that they are aware but want to be kept away from it. I'm pretty sure that Rob knows which is which. During the day, he'd occasionally say something like, *I wish the GM here had to live like these girls have to live.* In other cases, he'd say something derogatory about the Housekeeping Manager, which made me believe that the upper management at that hotel was not involved. I think when the Housekeeping Managers are on a bonus system for reducing expenses, which I think may be true at Fiesta Bay, they are rewarded by bonuses from the hotel as well as any kickbacks they might be getting from Trainor."

"I think you're right about Rob. He knows what's going on and does not like it. I hope he hasn't made his displeasure so obvious that he's put his life in danger. When you see Trevor tomorrow, be sure to protect Rob as best as you can. Tell Trevor that Rob did a great job indoctrinating you, but you still have some confusing areas. Tell him another round of deliveries with Rob might be needed for you to have a good handle on it."

"Sure. I think Trevor thinks I'm a 'dumb broad,' so he won't be surprised that I'm a little overwhelmed."

"Well, I could assure Trevor that you are anything but dumb, but for now, I'm glad that he thinks that way," Theresa said, giving Lucy a sly grin.

"While at the Fiesta Bay, I mentioned to Rob that I saw two names on the employee list for that hotel that seemed unusual and did not seem to be Hispanic. Rob said, '*I bet you mean Kishi. I saw her in the Housekeeping Manager's office on one of my visits. She seemed to be getting a reprimand. I saw the sad look on her face and felt so sorry for her. I don't know why she was being reprimanded, but the manager stopped when she saw me. After the girl left, I mentioned that this girl spoke English, which surprised me. The manager said, 'This stupid Indian thinks she was hired for a Hospitality job. I had to set Kishi straight, that's all.*'"

Sal said, "My pasta is ready. Let's take a break and chow down, but let's keep the recording going as well. You can keep throwing in details from the day while we enjoy our meal."

Lucy proceeded to go through the rest of the hotel visits, remembering many names and titles of the people introduced to her by Rob. In the end, she apologized for not remembering a few names, but Sal and Theresa were both amazed by her memory and complimented her on her recall. Lucy said, "I did ask Rob to give me a list of the names at each hotel. I told him I'd never remember everyone, and Rob said he would do that."

When the meeting was finished, Sal broke out a bottle of Malbec, knowing that was Lucy's favorite wine. The three shared the bottle and finished with some praise for Lucy's efforts, and discussed plans for the following day, hoping to protect Rob from any repercussions from Trainor Labor.

17

SAVING ROB

The next morning, Lucy was at her desk when Trevor came and asked her to come to his office. Lucy followed him down the hall to his office. Once there, he asked Lucy to take a seat. "So, how did things go yesterday with Rob? Did he do a good job of introducing you to the people and what needs to be done?"

"Rob did great, but trying to pack all that information into my brain from twelve clients, where to go, who to ask for, and so on, it was tough to remember everything. I'm sure after one more day with Rob, I'll have it all down perfectly."

"Oh, I see. I was hoping you'd be ready to do it all by yourself next week," Trevor said.

"If I had known you wanted that Trev, I should have kept written notes. It's not just our contacts and how to find their offices, but the personnel at the service entrances who I need to greet. If I walk in and someone who hasn't seen me before challenges my entering, I need to be able to explain who I'm there to see and who I met previously. Rob knows all those people, but I need at least one more trip to feel comfortable and not get kicked off the property."

"That's a good point. I never thought of that. I guess you're right. So, did you get along with Rob okay? I've heard that he tends to bitch about things."

"I certainly didn't see that side of him yesterday. I think he was trying to impress me. I got the feeling he might have been attracted to me, so he was on his best behavior. He treated me nice, but not actually hitting on me. That impressed me because I hate guys hitting on me." Lucy saw Trevor's macho side subside a little.

"Okay then, we'll keep Rob for one more week. We know he is looking for another job, so if you felt you were up to speed, we were going to let Rob go."

"Oh, I see. But I hate to be responsible for someone losing their job," Lucy said.

"I think this is a mutual decision. But don't mention it to Rob. Okay?"

"Not a problem. I've always been a loyal team player."

"I like hearing that," Trevor said. "Here's a new batch of invoices we need for some of our smaller clients in Ohio and small, rural towns around Erie. Maybe I can have you make these deliveries as well. I've been doing these myself, but I should spend more time in the office." Lucy thought that Trevor was just plain lazy, basically sitting in his office, visiting porn sites on his computer most of the time anyway, but having the opportunity to learn more about the operation sounded great to her.

It was lunchtime, and Lucy needed to run an errand at her bank. She wanted to know if it was okay to be gone for about an hour, Trevor didn't mind.

When Lucy got to her car in the small warehouse parking lot, there was a note sticking out from her side window. She grabbed the note and drove away, wondering what it could be about. No one frequented this part of the industrial area where she now worked, so it couldn't be some advertisement flyer. After driving a few blocks away from the office, Lucy pulled over to read the note. It read:

"Want to see how these girls have to live? I'm delivering food to the barracks today. Call me, Rob 814-555-1718."

Lucy called Theresa and read the note to her. "What should I do?" she asked Theresa.

"Call Rob and tell him you want to see the barracks, but you need to be back to work in an hour. This can be your chance to verify that Rob is truly an ally. Tell him you've talked to a friend about the situation and you may have some ideas on how to help the girls. If he shows interest, ask him if he'd like to discuss those ideas after work. In the meantime, I'll call Sal and see how he wants us to proceed."

"That's what I hoped you would say, Theresa. I'll call Rob and see if a quick visit to the barracks will work today. Should I take pictures?"

"Only snap some pics if the lady employees aren't around. Ask Rob if he's taken photos in the past. If so, ask him to bring them when we arrange a meeting. If you can get names from the lady employees, that would be a bonus, but don't be too obvious."

"Okay, Theresa. I'll call you on my way back to the office."

Lucy called Rob as soon as she hung up with Theresa. Rob answered with a careful "Hello," not sure that it was Lucy. Lucy said, "Hey, I got your note. I've got to be back to work in less than an hour. Is that enough time?"

"We can make it quick. I don't want to get you in trouble with Trevor. I wasn't sure if you left for lunch, but just took a chance after I heard your surprise over what I told you yesterday."

"Yes, I'm very interested, Rob. Where should I go?"

"I don't want you to drive your car in there. I've just picked up another load of over-ripe produce from that Warehouse Market around the corner from the office. If you come there, you'll see my pick-up around back. Drive back there, wave at me, and then park out in the parking area for the store. I'll pick you up and we can be back in about 45 minutes. Does that give you enough time?"

"I'm just two minutes from that Warehouse market. That timing should work out well to get me back to work in time. I'm already headed in your direction."

"See ya," Rob said.

Lucy saw Rob's green pick-up and waved as she drove by. Rob followed her out to the parking area and she jumped into Rob's truck after parking.

"I'm so glad you are interested in seeing this," Rob said. "I know this whole operation is wrong, but I've had nobody I could trust to discuss it with. Something needs to be done, but I'm all alone on this."

"From what you told me yesterday, I worried about it all last night. After I see it with my own eyes, I may have some ideas. Just where is this located?"

"It's in a small abandoned factory out behind the locomotive plant. There are a lot of small factories back there and only a few delivery trucks go back in there anymore, so they knew that nobody would see their vans coming in and out with the girls, to question what was going on. I think anyone who'd see them coming and going might think they are actually working there, rather than sleeping there."

"I can't wait to see it. I see all the old veggies in your truckbed. They don't look very fresh."

"The managers have deals with several of the big grocery stores to buy the stuff they normally discard or donate to charities. Most of this stuff would be turned down by the charities. When the girls get off work at the hotels, they have to sort through this stuff to find things that can be used for their meals."

"Do they get any protein, like meat or fish?" Lucy asked.

"Once a week I make the rounds to a few slaughterhouses to load up the pig and cattle guts. Sometimes they throw in some chicken hearts and gizzards if they have too much in stock. The girls make something like chitlins and they use the fat to cook with."

"I don't think I dare to take pictures today, but I was talking to a friend last night about what you told me, and I'd love to take pictures. She wasn't sure she believed what I was telling her."

"Don't you take any pictures? I'm going to tell the ladies we see there today that I needed help unloading things because I have other work to do today. So, try to just act like my helper and just keep your eyes open. I've taken pictures whenever I could, so I can share those with you later."

"That sounds right. I will try not to do anything that makes me look suspicious."

After we leave, I'll tell you about the women who are working there today. Some of them seem sympathetic to the girls, but some I don't trust. It's best that you just carry boxes and not say anything. I'll tell the women you are a new employee that I'm showing around, and you offered to help."

Rob drove behind a couple of larger abandoned factories and headed toward a small, three-story building at the end of the access road. He then drove to the back and up to a small loading dock. Rob hopped out of the truck and told Lucy to take the stairs up to the top of the dock, where Rob was tossing the boxes and bags of produce. Rob then hopped up to the dock, handed Lucy a couple of small plastic bags, and grabbed a large box for himself. They entered an industrial-looking door that led into what appeared to be a small warehouse. After proceeding down a short hallway, he turned a corner and came to an open area that had two old restaurant-style ranges with ovens and another with a flat grilling surface. Two old, stainless-steel coolers were on the back wall, which Lucy assumed would be a freezer and a refrigerator.

When he entered, Rob yelled, "It's Rob. I'm here with some food. Is anyone around?"

From around the corner, Lucy heard a response, and recognized a distinct Spanish accent, "Hi, Robbie! I'll be right there."

Rob turned to Lucy and quietly said, "Oh, good. This is Camila. She is one of the sympathetic ones. She tries her best to treat the girls with respect."

Camila came around the corner and showed little surprise when she saw Lucy with Rob. Camila said, "It's about time you got a girlfriend Robbie." She then greeted Lucy with, "Hola! Como estas! Me llamo, Camila."

Lucy responded, "Me llamo, Lucinda. Mis amigas me llamen Lucy. Mucho gusto, Camila!" Lucy looked over at Rob and saw his deep red blush. She then said, "We just introduced ourselves in Spanish. Why are you blushing?"

Camila said, "It's because I called you his girlfriend. Am I right?"

Lucy said, "Well I just met Rob yesterday, so maybe that's a bit early to assume. I just started working at the office this week and Rob was in a hurry today, so he asked me to help him with this delivery." When Lucy looked at Rob again, his blushing seemed to be even more pronounced than before. Camila also saw the blush on Rob's cheeks and looked over to Lucy, giving her a knowing wink. At that, Lucy gave Camila a big smile and winked back.

"Well, if you're in a hurry today, let me help you carry in the food. Did they give you anything decent this time?" Camila asked.

"The veggies are the normal junk, but I grabbed a couple of boxes of over-ripe fruit which looks decent. Yes, let's get the stuff inside. Who else is here today, Camila?"

"Just Lydia, the bitch! Sorry for my language, Lucy, but she is. She locked herself in with the night shift girls who were sleeping on the third floor. So, I'm doing laundry alone today. Do you have time to help me carry one big laundry cart up to the second floor, Robbie? I've asked the office three times to get that old elevator fixed, but Trevor just ignores me."

"Do you have time, Lucy? Lucy only had an hour to help me before she had to be back at work, so I don't want to get her into trouble."

"Let's get the food inside. I'm sure if I walk in ten minutes late, he won't be upset." "If you're talking about Trevor, please bug him about our elevator," Camila said.

Rob spoke up, "Trevor doesn't know that I asked Lucy to help me, so she'd better not let on that she was here today. He thinks she just took a lunch break. So, please don't mention that Lucy was helping me today. Okay, Camila?"

"Not a problem, you two. It's our secret," Camila answered, giving Rob a knowing smile, which made him blush again.

They quickly carried the last boxes of vegetables and fruit into the makeshift kitchen, and Camila led the way to the bottom of the stairs, where the huge rolling laundry cart was sitting. Rob said, "I think the stairs are wide enough here, so if you two ladies can handle one side, I'll take the other. Take it easy, one step at a time, setting the top wheels on each higher step. If you feel like it is too heavy, let me know."

Within just a couple minutes, they had made it up the 15 steps of the industrial-style stairway, and Camila rolled the cart down a short hallway into a large, open area that appeared to have been an assembly area for the old factory. Numerous old steel tables were shoved to one end, and the other three walls were covered by bunk beds that had been constructed using cheap, pine 2-by-4 lumber. Plywood had been used for the mattress support panels, and because Camila had stripped many of the bunks to wash the bedding, Lucy was shocked by what she saw being used as mattresses. Some actual twin mattresses were there, but they all had stains which appeared to be blood, urine, and worse.

"See what they expect my girls to sleep on?" Camila said. "I've asked that damn Trevor to get me some disinfectant, but he ignores me on that too!" she added, with obvious disdain in her voice. Then she added, looking at Lucy, "El es un pendejo, entiende usted?"

"I do understand, Camila. I think he's an asshole too, and I've only worked there less than a week."

Even Rob now understood, and the three of them laughed.

"We'd better quiet down, I don't want the bitch upstairs to hear us, and those girls need their sleep. Two of them came in this morning in tears. I think I know what's happening to them sometimes at work. I hear the other girls trying to console them."

And with that, Camila led them downstairs and out to the loading dock. She gave Rob a big hug and then turned to Lucy with her arms extended. Lucy came to Camila to accept the hug and Camila whispered in her ear, "Rob is a sweet guy. He would treat you right if you are interested." And then Camila kissed Lucy on the cheek.

"Can we do something to help my girls?" Camila asked as Rob and Lucy were getting into the truck.

Rob drove as quickly as possible to get Lucy back to her car, and Lucy said, "Now that I've seen that barracks, I understand how horrible the situation is. Did you understand what Camila was saying about the girls coming home crying, and needing consolation from the other girls?"

"That's the first time she's mentioned that to me, but I'm not sure if I understand. I think it means they are being abused or punished, but please tell me," Rob said, but with a look that made Lucy think he suspected what answer was coming.

"Camila suspects ~ and I do as well ~ that some of the girls are being used for sex, not just labor. When I discussed this with my friend last night, after seeing those invoices delivered through the service entrances of those hotels, my friend wondered if this was much more than a cheap labor operation. I think you'd love to meet my friend to discuss this situation further. Would you be willing to do that? She may have some ideas on how we can help them."

"I think I would like to meet her, as long as you'd be there as well."

"Of course, I'll be there. I think we're now a team. And that makes me ask, what do you know about Camila? Did they bring her in illegally too? Her English seems too good for me to believe that."

"No. Camila is a citizen. She came to the States about 20 years ago and worked in the vineyards. She married an American guy and they had one daughter. The daughter died of an overdose at just 16, and her husband committed suicide three months later. Camila almost did the same, but she realized she had a calling to help young girls stay away from the drugs that killed her daughter. She ended up homeless on the streets, but she's a real survivor. The other woman, Lydia, knew about her and that she was bi-lingual, so as much as Camila hates Lydia, it was Lydia who got her this job."

"I really loved her! She sure speaks her mind. That's for sure. Does she live at the barracks? I assume so if she is technically homeless."

"Oh yes, she stays with the girls and if it wasn't for Camila, I don't know if Lydia or the other two would ever do the laundry. They won't even help with the food. The two you didn't see today are also bilingual. They are older and live with their kids, somewhere around Erie. It's not that they are mean, like Lydia, but they seem to be afraid and are very quiet. I think they may be afraid of Lydia, unlike Camila who stands up to Lydia. I'm always worried that Camila could be fired, but I think that Trevor knows that Camila knows too much about the operation."

"That is a worry, which reminds me of something that my friend said last night. She said that organizations like this are very worried about someone reporting their illegal operation. So, she thought I should warn you to not be so open about your displeasure of what's going on around Trevor and his bosses. I assume that Trevor is not the big guy, right?"

"Right. I've only seen the other three guys a couple times that seem to get most of the money out of this. I was in the next room, which is now your office, one day when they came in. They were trash-talking about a couple of the girls, about them not cooperating at some party. They were real upset about someone called Yellowtail or Yellow-something."

"Yellowbird? She is another Native girl who works at the same hotel as Kishi."

"Yeah, Yellowbird. That was her. One guy said she'd better get with the program or they'd order a new one. He talked about her like she was a piece of meat."

"Well, I'm convinced that these guys don't think of them as human beings, that's for sure." "I'm so happy you could come with me today, Lucy. I feel so much better having shared my concerns with you. There's your car, so you'd better get back to the office."

"Yes, I have more invoices to prepare, and Trevor wants me to go along with him to deliver them tomorrow. I'm not working on Saturday. What about you?"

"No. They haven't asked me to gather more food tomorrow, and I only do that one invoice delivery run each week."

"Just wondering if we might get together and meet my friend to discuss our mutual concerns. I'll talk to her tonight and call you if you think it would be a good idea."

"I'd love to, Lucy. I hope she can help."

"Okay then. I'll call you tonight after I speak with her. And remember her advice of not being too negative around Trevor."

"That'll be tough. But I understand," Rob said, as he pulled up behind Lucy's car and let her out.

Lucy couldn't wait for her day to end so she could get home and talk to Theresa. She finished the new set of invoices. There were only eight this time, and the number of employees at each hotel was down to between 6 and 8, and not the 16 to 24 she had prepared for the larger hotels. Trevor reviewed the invoices and was complimentary about how well she had done. He told her he'd meet her in the office at 8:30 the following morning and they would deliver them together.

Lucy called Theresa on her way home and Theresa agreed that Sal would certainly want to hear more about Rob, and her surprise visit to the barracks where the girls were being kept.

Sal was waiting in her apartment building lobby, just like he had done the previous evening. "You could have gone up, Sal. No need to wait in the lobby," Lucy said.

"No, it's bad enough that we asked you to have Theresa stay with you during this investigation. I sent her up and said I'd wait here. I don't want to invade your privacy unnecessarily."

"Okay. If that's how you feel about it. I do appreciate how you've treated me during all of this. But let's get upstairs. Wait until you hear about my discoveries."

They were hit with the smell of another dinner being prepared as they entered Lucy's apartment. "What's cooking tonight?" Lucy asked.

"Well, I'm not the great cook that Sal seems to be, but I told him that I had a good recipe for Veal Marsala. How does that sound?" Theresa asked.

"I'm getting spoiled by you two. When I eat at home, it's usually frozen dinners or food from the grocery store Deli. That's why I was at those hotels near the marinas so often, mooching some good food."

"Well, I'm glad you were there, because it led to you helping us on this investigation. I do, however, hope that you've also learned how unsavory some of those people are, and how to avoid those situations in the future. I've grown to like you, Lucy, so my protective father side is showing. Understand?" Sal said.

"I do understand, and I do appreciate your concern. Really! This experience has me thinking. I'll tell you more about this guy, Rob, from today's experience, he's the first young guy I've ever met who doesn't keep hitting on me, and he actually blushed when the lady we met today mentioned something about me being his girlfriend. When we left that barracks, she whispered to me that Rob was a nice guy who would take care of me. I guess that before, I only considered a guy caring for me as taking me to dinner. Rob even opens doors for me. I'm not used to that."

"It sounds like he's too nice of a guy to be mixed up in this mess. We need to get him into protective custody as soon as we can," Theresa said.

"We'll get to that, but first, let's hear about Lucy's surprise visit to the barracks. I'll set up our digital recorder," Sal said.

Lucy started by telling them about the note on her car and meeting Rob at the Warehouse Grocery store where he picked her up. "You can't believe the stuff they are feeding those girls. They make the girls sort and clean the veggies and cook the food themselves. Today, Rob had a couple boxes of over-ripe fruit, which he said was unusual."

"What condition was the meat in, and how much do they have?" asked Sal.

"This place doesn't give them meat or fish," Lucy said incredulously. "Rob said that once a week, he visits a couple slaughterhouses where he gets, in his words, 'all the pig and cow guts.' The girls make chitlins, which my mom likes, but I hate. Rob also said they occasionally find some chicken gizzards and hearts thrown in, and they use the pork fat for cooking."

"Well, as bad as the chitlins sound, that's decent protein," Theresa said. "My kids would leave the table, but my ex-husband's family ate it regularly. He was from West Virginia, where it's pretty common in many families."

"Well, I guess you two are right," Lucy said. "Anyway, I have to tell you about the wonderful lady I met today. Her name is Camila, and she is a homeless widow who was recommended by one of the Anglo housemothers because Camila is bilingual. There are at least two other bilingual women that work there, but they go to their homes around Erie at the end of each day."

"Do you think Camila will be open to helping us?" Sal asked Lucy.

Before she could answer, he added, "Maybe we can use Camila's help once we close down the operation. Did you see any of the girls?"

"Camila said that the girls on the night shift sleep up on the third floor. Lydia, the nasty Anglo lady, sleeps up there as well. In talking to Camila, I got the impression that Lydia doesn't do much to help around the place. Camila was doing laundry, basically bedding, and we even helped her carry some up to the second floor. She said the elevator has been broken and her requests to have it fixed have been ignored by Trevor."

"So, in what kind of conditions are the sleeping areas?" Sal asked.

"Very rustic, with just wooden, hand-made bunk beds. The old steel tables from the previous factory are just shoved to one end. I think the girls, with help from Camila, and maybe the other bilingual ladies, are keeping it as sanitary as they possibly can, but the mattresses look like the discarded type I've seen at landfills. Some of them were uncovered because Camila was laundering the bedding, so I could see some old blood stains, urine stains, and so forth. Again, Camila said she's asked for disinfectant, but Trevor ignores her."

"Anything else you want to add before we eat?" Theresa asked. "My veal is ready."

"Just something that Camila said about some of the girls coming home crying, and the others trying to console them. She gave me a concerned, knowing look, and I think she realized that these girls have been used for sex. I don't think that Rob had realized that fact before today. Later, he mentioned overhearing something specific about Yellowbird. He thought they were just going to reprimand her for something, but one of the bosses in that meeting said, "If she doesn't get with the program, we'll need to replace her. I get the feeling that she is not cooperating when they use her at sex parties."

"It sounds like we need to move as quickly as we can. Do we know all of the hotel clients now?" Sal asked.

"Oh yes, I have pictures of the invoices for the eight I prepared today. I'm going along with Trevor tomorrow to deliver them. These are all small, privately owned hotels, with three smaller chain hotels. That makes it twenty clients, and I believe that may be all of them. Trevor mentioned some locations in New York and Ohio, but those accounts are handled by others."

"Do you think there could be other places where they are keeping the girls at night?" Sal asked.

"I'm assuming that Rob is the only one delivering food, and this is the only place he knows about," Lucy answered. "And I did broach the subject of Rob meeting with us. I just said that I'd mentioned his concerns to a friend. I think Rob wants to help and I suggested a meeting on Saturday. Is that okay that I suggested it? I want to get Rob out of that situation as soon as we can. If they know that he is not happy, and with as much as he knows, I'm worried about his safety, after you mentioned that they could possibly have him killed."

"Yes, I think it's time to get him out of there. I'll call my Station Chief in Pittsburgh and see if he agrees. We can either have Rob just disappear, or we can make it look like he's been arrested. Can you call Theresa tomorrow around late morning? I'll have an answer by then. If Rob happens to talk to you, tell him your friend wants to meet him on Saturday."

"That's great. Thanks, Sal," Lucy said. "How about at Valerio's? Maybe after the lunch rush is over."

Sal agreed to meet her there.

After Sal left on Thursday evening, Lucy called Rob's cell phone to find out if he could talk with her for a few minutes.

"Sure, Lucy. Good to hear from you."

Lucy jumped right to it, "I spoke with my friend after getting home from work. She has some good advice for both of us concerning this mess we've found ourselves in. Can we get together sometime on Saturday to talk about it?"

"I was hoping you'd call," Rob said, sounding relieved. "After seeing your reaction to the food and living conditions of the girls out at the warehouse, I've been thinking that I just can't be part of this anymore. I'm not doing anything to hurt those girls, but I just can't keep ignoring it either."

"Great," Lucy said. "Let's meet somewhere for lunch, away from the hotels or anywhere that we might be seen together. Do you know where Valerio's restaurant is, over on the West side?" "Sure. I've never been inside, but I drive by the place occasionally. What time?" "Let's avoid the big lunch rush. How about two o'clock?"

"I'll be there." Then pausing briefly, Rob sounded sincere when he added, "Thanks a lot, Lucy. I'm so happy that you feel like I do."

"Am I detecting more than a professional tone in your voice, my friend?" Theresa teased Lucy when she got off the phone. "It seems like you've quickly developed a lot of respect for Rob. What are you thinking?"

Lucy blushed. "He's just a normal guy, Theresa. He's nice-looking, but not a stud. I've always been attracted to the studs, but look where that got me, doing one-night stands for a nice dinner. Those guys don't open doors and don't blush when someone asks about me being their girlfriend. In fact, I can see that Rob is attracted to me, but he turns away and looks guilty when I catch him looking at me. And unlike the old joke, he is always stealing looks at my face, not at my boobs."

"It sounds like Rob is a good guy. When this operation is over, maybe you need to turn your investigation toward Rob. Has that thought crossed your mind?"

"I guess I've been trying to ignore that possibility. But in a matter of just 48 hours, I can't seem to get him off my mind. I've been telling myself that it was just concern for his safety, but now that you've put it into words, I'm wondering if you could be right."

"You deserve to find a good man, Lucy. Even if Rob isn't the guy of your dreams, I think he is a good step in the right direction."

18

WORKING WITH TREVOR

On Friday morning, Trevor was already in his office when Lucy arrived. "Thanks for being on time, Lucy. These hotels are scattered out in the suburbs, so it will take much of the day to make my deliveries. I don't know if you kept notes on the day you spent with Rob, but I think you will need to do that today. Some of these smaller places are off the beaten path."

"I didn't keep written notes on that day with Rob. That's why I think I need to make one more delivery trip with him, to be sure that I don't make any mistakes."

"Well, we'll see how that works out. But grab a pad of paper to make notes today, and let's get going."

The deliveries varied even more than they had at the larger hotels. Lucy didn't feel that the management was nearly as involved, as long as the work got done. She also spotted many of the girls who were doing the laundry and cleaning the rooms. Generally, they seemed to be the older, and less attractive girls. Lucy thought that these smaller hotels were not involved with the sex trade like they were at the larger hotels where the conventioneers and yachters stayed.

When Trevor was not within earshot, she would give a Spanish greeting to the girls, receiving a few cautious smiles in return, but none of them greeted her back. They had probably been warned not to be very friendly. At two hotels, Trevor asked her to wait in the lobby while he met with the manager. Lucy suspected that those meetings were to discuss girls being used for sex, so she made mental notes to mention that to Teresa.

The last hotel of the day was not a real hotel, but just a run-down old motel. It had several pick-up trucks in front of the rooms, and several had a barbecue grill out front. Lucy recognized it as one of the places serving itinerant construction workers, staying for a week or more at a time. Trevor introduced Lucy to the owner, a guy called Rex.

"Have you brought me some new talent, Trev?" Rex said when he saw Lucy. "She'll be a great addition."

Lucy cringed. And for a split second, she was overtaken by fear. What if Trevor had tricked her into coming with him to this place to leave her with Rex?

"No, Lucy is my new timekeeper. She'll be making my weekly deliveries from now on." Lucy felt the blood returning to her drained body. She scowled at Rex.

"Too bad," Rex said, leering at her. "She's a real looker."

"You've got five nice ones, Rex. Don't get greedy," Trevor said, turning to look from Rex to Lucy with a smirk on his face.

"How's Gabriela working out?" Trevor asked Rex. All three of them were now standing in the small lobby of the motel, the scent of burnt cigarette ashes and cheap cologne filling the air.

"She's a good worker but the guys never give her a second look."

"Well, that leaves more time for the others to make you money, right?" Trevor said, laughing.

Lucy looked around. There wasn't much foot traffic like there was at the larger hotels. The young man behind the counter wore a bored look on his face as he silently browsed on his phone, and there was a young lady drying clothes on a clothesline behind the office building. She could see her through the glass side door.

Lucy remembered that the timecards for this client showed the little stars most days for five of the girls employed at this location. The conversation between Trevor and Rex confirmed her suspicions about this location. Their main business here was to sell the girls' services to satisfy the workers' sexual appetites.

"Just ignore old Rex," Trevor said on the drive back to the office. "He spends too much time alone and he tends to talk nonsense. Don't let it bother you."

Lucy wondered how Trevor could think that his comment about Gabriela leaving more time for the others to make money for Rex, could mean anything other than what she suspected. Were the other employees that naïve, and did Trevor think that she was oblivious to what was going on? Other than Rob and Camila, why were the other employees keeping their mouths shut? How could they know that these girls were being abused, and just ignore the situation?

When she was finally alone, Lucy called Theresa and suggested another meeting with Sal, to discuss what had happened that day. When she arrived home, Sal was again waiting for her in the lobby. Lucy was beginning to find it as a compliment, with Sal respecting her privacy.

"So, young lady, I assume that this was another eye-opening day?" Sal said.

"Wait until you hear. Very different from the deliveries to the large hotels."

"Lead the way," Sal said.

As they sat at their usual positions, again watching Sal do the cooking, Lucy's first statement was a question, "How can Trevor show me these terrible things and assume that I don't have a conscience? I've only been here for a week, and he just assumes that I don't care about what's going on. Of course, he doesn't know that I've seen the barracks and that I've talked with Rob and Camila about other details, but today, he and a guy named Rex were talking about five of the girls working there being used for sex. Rex was hoping that Trevor had brought me out there as 'new talent.'"

"I think the mentality of these people is that everyone works for money, Lucy," Sal said. "They don't really care what you think, but if they pay you well, you won't jeopardize your job, and you'll just keep your mouth shut, or ignore the obvious. What makes it sad is that they are right about most people. And if they discover a threat, like Rob, they would not hesitate to make him disappear."

"That reminds me, Sal. I mentioned needing another week with Rob to be sure I fully understood those deliveries," Lucy said. "Trevor initially said, 'We'll see how that works out,' when I brought it up, and I didn't like the sound of that."

"I think you read that right, Lucy. Rob's displeasure with what they are doing has been noticed. I spoke with my Station Chief today, and he suggested that we don't wait until tomorrow to get Rob into protective custody. Can you call him now and invite him to come here for dinner? We've made enough beef stroganoff for four."

Lucy smiled and grabbed her phone. Rob answered the phone on the second ring. "Are you free

tonight?" Lucy asked him. "Change of plans. My friend is here for dinner and wants to meet you." Rob sounded surprised but also pleased. "I have no plans. I'd love to. Where?"

Lucy gave him her address. "I'll just change and get going. I can be there in fifteen minutes," Rob said, and then quickly hung up.

Lucy continued giving details about the other stops she had made with Trevor, explaining, "I remembered from the time sheets for these clients that other than the small motel which I'll save for last, only two locations had girls with the tell-tales X's after their times. The last place was a run-down motel, which looked like it catered to the longer-stay, itinerant construction workers. The conversation between Trevor and this Rex guy became obvious that he is using five of the girls primarily as sex-for-sale. I only saw one of the girls there, as she was hanging laundry behind the office, and she seemed to be more mature than I expected. I wonder if they find girls who had on-the-street experiences back home and use them in places like this. I don't think Rex cared if they could clean the rooms, as long as they didn't argue when the workers wanted them for the night."

"I'm sure you're right," Theresa said. "We can't expect that everyone they've convinced to come north is innocent and in-experienced. They probably treat these girls a little better, feed them better and give them enough perks to keep them happy. If you saw one of the women hanging laundry, I suspect that they are not transported back and forth to that barracks, but live right there at the motel. If they are treating them well, they are staying willingly."

"What will INS do with those girls?" Lucy asked.

"I assume that those women may not wish to stay in the U.S.," Sal answered. "They would be expected to give up pros-titution, which is the only life they probably know. If they want to change and find a normal job, I'm sure it will be con-sidered, but those will be tough cases. I didn't think that we would find cases like this. It's a sad situation for them."

Sal, Theresa, and Lucy discussed the events of the day for fifteen minutes and then they heard the entrance door buzzer ring. Lucy got up and hit the intercom. It was Rob. Lucy let him up and went to the door to meet him. To her own sur-prise, she hugged Rob. "Welcome, "she said, "Let me intro-duce you."

Lucy noticed the blush on Rob's cheeks, caused by her hug, and she was again impressed. She then turned to Theresa and Sal and said, "Guys, this is Rob. The fella I've been telling you about. Rob, this is my friend, Theresa, and her friend, Sal."

Theresa and Sal both walked over to Rob and shook his hand. "I'm Sal Dominico. What's your last name, Rob? I don't think that Lucy ever mentioned it."

"It's Brankovic, Robert Brankovic. Third generation Croatian."

"I've been to Croatia a few times. Beautiful country, great people, and fantastic food. Have you ever been there, Rob?"

"No, but it's on my bucket list. That's for sure. My grandparents came over shortly after World War II. They were from a small inland town, but they always raved about the Adriatic Coast, the great wine, and how much they missed the Croatian olive oil."

"I know," said Sal. "The olive oil from the Dalmatian region tastes like you are eating the actual olives. Just wonderful. Theresa, why don't you get to know Rob a bit better? I have to get something that I forgot in my car."

Sal had managed to put Rob at ease. Lucy noticed this and smiled at Sal.

Sal went to his car, but he had an ulterior motive. He called the Pittsburgh office and asked for Alex. "Hey, Alex. Sal Dominico here. Would you run the name Robert Brankovic for me, including parents, grandparents, and any siblings? He lives here, in Erie. Send it to my phone as soon as possible, if you would."

"I'm on it, Sal. Probably in ten, fifteen minutes at the most."

"That's great. Thanks, Alex."

Sal went back to the lobby and buzzed Lucy's apartment. Theresa buzzed him in.

Lucy and Rob seemed to be in a deep conversation when Sal walked back into the apartment. Theresa smiled at Sal and then lifted a finger to her lips, telling him not to talk.

When Lucy finally saw that Sal was back, she said, "I just learned that Rob is two years into his degree in Computer Science at the University. He took a break to make some money but plans to go back to school next year. He graduated from the same high school as I did, just two years ahead of me."

"That's fantastic," Sal said. "What do your parents do for a living, Rob?"

"They run a small Mom & Pop grocery store on the East side of town. It's in the Slavic neighborhood, and my dad makes his own Croatian sausages to sell in the store. I just have one sister, and she helps in the store. She's engaged to a fella who has worked in the store for a few years, so I think my dad is planning on turning the store over to them eventually. I told my dad when I went to college that I wasn't interested in running the store, so it works out."

"We have a lot of those little, ethnic grocery stores around Pittsburgh. I love to stop at them for their great homemade pastries, and I have tried some sausages, probably like the ones your dad makes. I think dinner is about ready, so let's get seated. I see that Theresa has set the table, so we're eating fancy tonight."

At that moment, Sal's cell phone chimed. "Why don't you all get seated and start with the rolls? I'll check this text message and get the stroganoff on the table." Sal stepped away and opened his text. He read it and smiled. When he turned toward the table, Theresa met his gaze while Lucy and Rob remained in serious conversation. Sal smiled at Theresa and gave her the thumbs up, and Theresa smiled widely in return.

Sal served the meal and the four of them began to eat. "You know Theresa is a friend of Lucy's, but I'm surprised that you haven't questioned why I'm here, Rob," Sal said, looking at Rob from across the dining table.

"Well, I might be curious, but if you're a friend of Lucy's, then I'm not concerned because I trust her."

Sal nodded. "We also trust Lucy's evaluation of you, which is why we asked you here. Lucy has told us what you've told her and shown her about that Trainor Labor Company. Can we just lay our cards out on the table for you?"

"Of course," Rob said. "Lucy knows that I'm not happy with what I think is going on, but I don't know what I can do to change it. If the big guys knew how I thought about it, they wouldn't be happy."

"That's why Lucy told us she was worried about your safety, Rob. She gets the feeling that Trevor knows about your attitude, and the organization may want to silence you."

"By silence, I think you mean they might kill me? Do you think they would go that far?" Rob asked.

"Oh, yes. This is a pretty sophisticated international organization, and there is a lot of money being made, selling these girls for labor and sex. If you're a threat to them, they would have no second thoughts about making you disappear."

"So, what can I do?" Rob asked, surprisingly showing little emotion.

"I guess it's my turn to be honest with you, Rob. I'm a Special Agent with the FBI, and Theresa is also an FBI Agent. Lucy reported a suspicious incident at one of the hotels involving young women who she suspected to be illegals being used for sex. We recruited Lucy to work with us as an insider, getting enough information to eventually shut the operation down, and rescue the girls. To be very honest, because Lucy met you early into her employment at Trainor Labor, and you have been so forthcoming with information, we think we can expedite the sting on this operation much sooner than expected. However, we now fear for your safety, and we want to take you into protective custody. From things that Lucy has heard from this Trevor guy, they are worried about your loyalty and are probably afraid of you doing exactly what's happening right here."

Rob looked at Lucy and said, "You were worried about me? I was worried about you too, but I was afraid that you didn't care about the girls. That was until I saw yesterday at the barracks, that you do care."

"So, I need to ask you, Rob," Sal said. "First, are you willing to disappear on short notice? By that, I mean, tonight. I don't want these guys to get to you, and I think my concern is real and imminent. And second, are you willing to cooperate with us in the investigation, and eventually testify against those in the organization?"

"Other than the fact that I only have the clothes on my back, I can disappear. My parents tend to call me on Sunday to check on me, but otherwise, I have no responsibilities, other than paying my rent. I do have a cat though. Somehow, I need to take care of Fuzzy."

"I've always wanted a cat," Lucy said. Is Fuzzy a boy or a girl?

"A very temperamental, neutered male. Just feed and water him, and keep the litter box clean, and he's happy. Once a day, usually evening, he comes and sits in my lap. Pet him for five minutes and he leaves. He's very little trouble, which is why he and I get along."

Lucy nodded, and then Rob turned back to Sal. "So, what did you have in mind?"

"I think we'll make it look like you were arrested, so we can gather some evidence from your apartment, which will include a lot of clothing. The arresting officers would typically interview your parents and sister. They will explain the protective custody situation and ask them to keep it secret. I assume that they will understand?"

"My mom and dad are cool cucumbers. Typical, stoic Croatians! They'll do whatever you ask. And they can handle my sister. She and I are on great terms." Rob said.

Theresa, who had been listening and nodding to the back and forth between Sal and Rob, finally chimed in. "Let's talk about the people you know at that barracks and who can be trusted. We know about Camila, and that Lydia is not very compassionate. What do you know about the other women who work there?"

"I think they are decent people, just afraid of making waves. They probably need the money, plus they may be afraid of what would happen to them if they reported any-thing. They probably have friends who are illegals, and they probably don't realize just how abused these girls are. Camila, on the other hand, has experienced losing her daughter, and is more aware and concerned."

"What happened to her daughter?" Theresa asked.

Lucy looked solemnly at Rob before telling Theresa and Sal that Camila's daughter had died, at the age of 16, from a drug overdose, and that her husband killed himself just three months later. "That's so sad," Theresa simply said.

"Yes, it is," Lucy agreed.

Sal and Rob simply nodded.

"Have you met any of the people above Trevor?" Sal asked after a quick pause. "Do they come to the office regularly?"

"They usually come to the office once every two weeks, al-ways on a Wednesday, when I am gone on deliveries. Trevor makes sure that I'm not in the office when they come. I think that is when they come for their share of the profits. I told Lucy about them being there once when I was still at the of-fice. They were upset about that girl, Yellowbird."

"When was the last time they were in the office, Rob?" asked Sal.

"Last week. The week before Lucy started."

"So, that means this coming Wednesday is our day. Lucy will probably make the rounds of the big hotels on Wednes-day. Do you have any idea how the payments are made to Trainor?"

"Not really. I have seen Trevor counting cash and going to the bank. I just thought that was his own money."

"I can't believe that the labor invoices are paid in cash. Even at this ridiculously low hourly rate, the hotels need a record of payments for labor to a contractor. However, those extra red Xs that Lucy has seen, may certainly be handled in cash. That's what those guys come to collect every two weeks. I doubt that other than those red X's, there is no written record of those."

Pondering the discussion, Rob was beginning to realize just how deep this organization's illegal activities ran. Looking around the room, he said, "Until yesterday, I think I was pretty naïve. How did I not know that some of the girls were being forced to have sex as part of their job? I heard Camila and Lucy referring to them being consoled by the others, but it never even crossed my mind. I'm so dumb sometimes."

"Don't be so hard on yourself," Lucy said, reaching over and touching Rob's shoulder reassuringly. "You couldn't have known."

"Yes," Theresa chimed in, "What's important is that you still spotted the overall problem. We thank you for that, just like Lucy spotting it at that hotel."

"One thing we still don't know, Rob. Do you know how they are transporting the girls to the hotels and back?" Sal asked Rob.

"Camila told me once that a couple of the small hotels are picking up the girls with the hotel shuttle vans. You know, the ones they pick up guests with from the airports. But Trainor has some deal with an outfit called Apostolic Baptist Ministries. I've seen a couple of old, beat-up buses out at the barracks a couple times. That name is on the side of the bus. The buses look like they hold about thirty people. I think those buses deliver the girls to the large hotels."

"Let me call my buddy who lives on his computer. I'll have him check that out," Sal said.

"Oh, wait," Rob said, "Lucy asked to see any pictures I had taken at the barracks. I didn't want her taking pictures in case someone besides Camila was around. I know I took a picture of one of those buses."

"That would be very helpful," said Sal.

Rob took out his phone and looked through his photo gallery, then said, "Here it is," and handed his phone to Sal.

"Wow! You have the license plate in this picture. Can I forward this picture to my buddy? He's another Agent, but he's probably home, back in Pittsburgh."

"Of course," Rob said. "I have several other pictures in there that you may want to have."

Sal sent the picture from Rob's phone to himself and then forwarded it to his friend in Pittsburgh. Sal then asked Rob for permission to look at his other photos, and as they were doing so, Sal's phone rang.

Sal answered his phone, saying, "Hey, Chet. That was fast. What did you find?" I'm putting you on speaker so the others can hear. Okay?"

"That's fine, Sal," Chet said. "That bus is no longer owned by Apostolic Baptist Ministries. That license plate is registered to a company called TL Transport. I checked them out and it appears to be owned by Trainor Labor Company. Isn't that the outfit you're investigating?"

"It sure is. Thanks, Chet. No rush on this, but tomorrow, could you look into Trainor Labor and see if you can find any financials, banking information, and any people associated with them? If you find any other companies owned by them, that would be very helpful."

"I'll get on it first thing in the morning, Sal," Chet said. "Have a good evening. Is that Theresa I heard in the background? Hi, Tess. How's Erie?"

"The best thing about Erie is the great friends we've found here. You may get to meet them soon," Theresa said. "Thanks for the info, Chet. Good night."

"Good night, everyone," Chet said, hanging up the phone.

"So, your nickname is Tess?" Lucy asked. "I wondered about that but was afraid to ask if you used that."

"My friends all call me Tess, except at work. You now qualify as a friend, so please call me Tess if you prefer."

"Thanks, Tess. I will if you don't mind."

"Hey, if you are placing me under arrest tonight, what happens next?" Rob asked as if he had been thinking about it for a while. "Am I going to jail, or what?"

Sal and Theresa laughed. "Not really. If you understand why we are doing this, and you are in agreement, we will present you with a Writ stating that you are being placed in protective custody. We can't just check you into a hotel, because most, if not all of the hotels are involved in this Trainor business. So, assuming that you would agree, we've rented a small apartment for you to use as your Safe House. I think we will be launching our sting within the next few days, so you won't have to stay there too long. If you agree, I have a team ready to gain entry into your current apartment, purportedly looking for evidence. They will gather most of your clothes and any personal items you'd like us to bring to you. You'll have a guy staying in the apartment, 24 hours, for security. They'll not sleep, and they'll work in shifts."

"Wow! You think the Trainor guys are that serious?" Rob asked.

"I believe that you were already in danger, just based on what Trevor said to Lucy this afternoon. But once the word gets out that you've been arrested, they are going to assume the worst. That's why we need to act fast, and we're planning on it happening on Wednesday when Lucy is delivering those invoices. We are calling in Agents from several stations, so that as Lucy delivers each invoice, we will have two Agents there to arrest the person taking the invoice. That person may not be the one making decisions for that hotel, but they will be interrogated to find the others."

"What about the girls?" Rob asked.

"Apparently, the majority of the girls are delivered to the hotels between 0600 and 0700 each morning. As those old church buses leave the barracks that morning, the driver will be arrested, and the girls will be returned to the barracks for their safety. If the bus was to pick up any girls who worked the night shift, we'll have the driver make his rounds to pick them up, and safely return them to the barracks. We will also intercept any hotel buses that come to the location of the barracks. We doubt that the hotel drivers are criminally involved, and they will cooperate with us once they understand what's happening. I'm thinking that they were curious, but kept their mouth shut, thinking their jobs could be at stake."

"Will we be able to warn Camila before this happens?" Lucy asked.

"Sal and I have discussed that earlier today. Does Camila have a cell phone, Rob?" Theresa

asked.

"If she does, I've never seen her use it," Rob answered.

"Do you know Camila's last name?" Theresa asked Rob.

"I don't. But maybe we can find it in the newspaper articles about her daughter and husband's deaths. They both occurred two years ago."

"Great idea," Sal said. "That's another thing for Chet to work on tomorrow morning. Once we know that, we can find her cell phone number, and we'll have you make a call to warn her. She will be a big help once we get all the girls back to that barracks and under one roof."

"What about those small hotels that I visited with Trevor?" Lucy asked.

"Once the girls are brought back, other than those from that one small motel being used as a brothel, who probably live there, we will visit each hotel and try to determine how involved they are in the operation. From what you've seen, Lucy, they may only be using the girls for cheap labor, other than that one. We will still file charges and investigate their involvement, but other than us rescuing the girls from the slave labor situation, the hotels may not have anything illegal going on. But to avoid them hiding any records if the word gets around about our Wednesday arrests, do you think you can make those small hotel deliveries on Thursday?"

"I can tell Trevor that I need Friday off. I see no reason why I can't make those deliveries early."

"Fantastic," Sal said. "As soon as you leave the Trainor office to start your deliveries, we plan to move in. We'll arrest Trevor and seize all the records on-site. I think Rob believed that the other Trainor management came to the office every second Wednesday. Is that right, Rob?"

"Yes. They should be there this coming Wednesday if their schedule is consistent."

"Then we'll be there to arrest them when they arrive. They won't be warned if we act fast."

"Okay, so once the girls are safe at the barracks, what happens to them?" Lucy asked.

"This is where our friend, Liz, at the DA's office gets involved. She's organized that local women's shelter and several good bilingual counselors to assist, and that lady you met from INS has also prepared Spanish-speaking staff to come to Erie. I understand that Liz has also contacted several local food pantries to supply food for the girls until we get them interviewed and placed in separate homes or shelters. Liz has been working on this ever since we met with her at the DA's office, and she keeps emphasizing that these girls need to be treated as victims, and with tenderness, and not accusing them like criminals. They were duped by the people who recruited them, and they are the victims. We do not want them to think that we are treating them as criminals."

"And when do you plan on having me arrested?" Rob asked.

"We'd do it here, but just in case you are being watched by the Trainor people, I've told the team to be at your apartment when you get home tonight. They will meet you outside and take you away in handcuffs, then impound your car and search your apartment, to make it look real. They will take you to the County Jail, but will lead you out the back to the apartment we rented for your safety. We've already stocked the refrigerator for you and picked the agents who will be staying with you," Sal answered.

Rob nodded. "If this is what it takes to put an end to this, then I'm ready. This situation troubled me as soon as I figured out what was going on. And as much as I wanted to do something, I was afraid that the girls could be hurt if I acted prematurely. Will they also take Fuzzy into custody?"

"Well, it was just a lucky break that you were sent with Lucy on that first invoice delivery. If you had vented to someone loyal to Trevor, you might have been eliminated sooner," Theresa said. "But what about Fuzzy?"

Lucy quickly spoke up, "Can you bring Fuzzy over here? I'd love to take care of him!" Sal said, with a smile, "I'll deliver Fuzzy here myself, later tonight."

With a plan in place and everyone assigned their duties in how this sting was going to be put into effect, Rob departed from Lucy's apartment alone that night. He drove home and thought about the events that would soon be set into motion and he felt his heart pounding heavily in his chest. He knew he was not going to jail, but the thought of it all still filled him with dread.

19

GETTING READY FOR THE STING

Lucy returned to work on Monday to find Trevor was already there. He beckoned her into his office and handed her three envelopes containing the latest timecards for the large hotels. Lucy took the envelopes and was on her way out of his office when he stopped her with a question.

"Hey, Lucy, have you seen Rob?"

Lucy stopped at the door and turned to face Trevor.

"No, I've not," she simply said.

"Hmmm...do you know where he is? He's not shown up for work and he's not answering his phone."

"That's strange. I haven't heard from him since he left my apartment on Friday evening."

Seeing Trevor's eyebrows curve upwards, Lucy quickly added that Rob had come to her apartment thinking he could start a romantic relationship with her. She assured Trevor that she'd let him down gently, but finally told him he had to leave because she was not interested in a relationship with him. That was the last time she'd heard from Rob.

If Trevor questioned how Rob knew where she lived, he did not verbalize it. Instead, he said, "I've wondered about that guy's intentions. He's been acting weird these last few weeks. I think I may need to fire him sooner than planned. Can you make those deliveries alone on Wednesday? You said that you needed Rob to go along with you again this week, but it looks like you'll have to do that without him."

"Oh sure," Lucy said. "It might take me a bit longer to find my way to the right office at each place, but I can do it. No problem."

"Great. You're working out well, Lucy. So, get started on these invoices and I need to find Rob, so I can break the news to him. I need to find someone new to do our supply runs, otherwise, I'll be doing that as well on Tuesdays and Thursdays. That damn Rob has screwed up my schedule."

"Okay, Trevor. I'll get going on these invoices. Will I also be making deliveries to those small hotels? Is it possible that I could do those on Thursday this week? I was going to ask if I could take Friday off for a doctor's appointment. I had forgotten about that appointment until they called to remind me last Friday."

"Sure. No problem. I'll get those timecards ready for you later today."

"Thanks, Trev. I appreciate it."

Lucy sent Theresa a quick text as soon as she got to her desk.

Lucy: *Trevor is looking for Rob*

Theresa: *That was to be expected, how did that conversation go?*

Lucy told Theresa what she had said to Trevor. She also told Theresa that she had switched Friday's deliveries to Thursday. Doing this would hopefully prevent word from getting out to the hotels about the arrests made at the larger harbor-front hotels. Lucy had informed Sal and Theresa that the smaller hotels didn't seem to be aware that some of their operations were illegal, but they still wanted to catch those managers off guard.

Lucy quickly finished working on the new invoices and took them to Trevor for approval. Once approved, Trevor handed her the envelopes with timecards for the smaller hotels.

"Great. I'll get started on these before I leave for today. I'll finish them tomorrow morning, and I'll be ready to make deliveries on Wednesday and Thursday," Lucy said, taking the envelopes from Trevor.

"You're a fast worker, Lucy. Much more efficient than our last girl. Maybe we can catch a dinner on Friday, so I can show my gratitude."

"That might be nice," Lucy responded, knowing she'd never go to dinner with Trevor, even under the best circumstances. Of course, she also knew that Trevor would be in County Jail by Wednesday. "I'll hold Friday night open. Have you heard from Rob, by the way?"

"He has totally disappeared," Trevor said. "No answer on his phone, and I sent our bus to his apartment. He doesn't answer the door, and his car is gone. Good riddance, I guess."

THE STING

Lucy arrived early at the office on Wednesday morning. She wanted to get an early start in case she had any trouble with finding directions to all the hotels. She told that to Trevor who said she could call him if she had any trouble.

"I'll be here all day with an important meeting," Trevor added.

"Oh. So that I don't interrupt your meeting by calling you, what time will it be taking place?" Lucy asked.

"The guys usually show up around ten," Trevor replied. "But if you have any questions, just call. They won't mind the interruption. You are part of the meeting's agenda anyway. I've told my boss how well you are doing, and they are thinking about expanding your role in the business."

"That's nice to hear, Trevor, thanks for the compliment," Lucy said.

Lucy departed the office about 30 minutes later, but first, she went to the restroom to gather herself, and then she sent a quick text message to Theresa and Sal to confirm the meeting time. Lucy said that she was worried about going into the hotel before Trevor was arrested, in case someone in the hotel might call Trevor.

Theresa was at the local Field Office with Sal when they received Lucy's text. They advised Lucy to stall the deliveries until they could get to the operations office and arrest the bosses. They didn't want someone from the hotel tipping them off, like Lucy had mentioned.

"Position yourself near your first stop, the Fiesta Bay, and as soon as they have Trevor and the others in custody, Sal will call you to have you start the deliveries," Theresa's text message read. *"Sal said to thank you for thinking like that. Maybe you need to become a permanent part of the team."*

Lucy wondered if the FBI would be a good career path for her. It was amazing how her perception of Law Enforcement had changed in such a short time.

Two blocks away from the Fiesta Bay Hotel, Lucy parked her car and nervously kept an eye on her phone. She knew that the two Agents who would meet her at the hotel were also waiting to receive Sal's message to start, but she had no idea where they were located.

At just a little after 10:15 am, Lucy's phone rang. It was Sal. "Trevor and three others are in custody, Lucy. It was funny to hear Trevor after we read him his rights. The only thing he said was, 'That damn Rob.' I guess he knew and I'm glad we got Rob protected as soon as we did. He never mentioned you, so you did great, and I doubt that he suspects you at all. So, now, head to Fiesta Bay, the agents are watching for your car. When they make the arrests, they will have a county sheriff outside to transport them. They will then follow you to your next delivery and make arrests there also. The County Sherrif will shuttle several squads from your hotel stops to the jail, in order to keep the operation running."

"It sounds like you've been busy with these details over the weekend, Sal. It seems very well organized," Lucy said.

"Thanks to you, Lucy. You're thinking like an agent already! If we run into any snags or delays, my agents will tell you, and you can just wait a little longer between deliveries. So, head to Fiesta Bay. Theresa just told me that the agents are waiting for you, just outside the street leading into the service entrance."

"Did all go well at the barracks this morning? Are all of the girls okay?" Lucy asked.

"We stopped the buses as they picked up the girls," Sal said. "We're also coordinating the pick-up of the night shift girls to coincide with your visits. You may find the hotels are upset that the girls have not arrived for the day shift. So, as we discussed last night, tell them that Trevor told you that one of the buses had broken down. As soon as you hand them the invoice, our agents will be making the arrests, so the excuse is just to get you out of the hotel without any drama. I know that you are wearing the wire, so I'm curious to hear the hotel personnel's reactions."

"I understand," Lucy said. "I just parked in the Fiesta Bay service area. I see a big black car pulling in behind me, so I assume those are your agents. And right behind them, I just spotted a Sherrif's squad car. Is it okay if I'm feeling a bit nervous?"

"I'd wonder what was wrong with you if you said you weren't nervous. Thank you for being part of our team, Lucy. At the end of the day, you will know you've saved these women from hell on earth. Then we just have to deal with the less threatening locations tomorrow."

"I'm just worried about the girls in that small motel. I think they knew what they were coming here to do."

"Not everyone we find in these situations is innocent, Lucy. They may be the ones who request to be sent home. We'll deal with the situation and decide what is best for them. We cannot allow them to continue if that is their chosen profession. I'm not looking forward to that part of the operation either," Sal answered. "It's hard for us to understand what it takes just to survive in some 3rd world countries. I don't want to judge them."

"Okay Sal, your guys are walking towards my car. I guess it's time to put on my game face. Talk to you later."

Lucy walked through the employee entrance at the rear of the hotel. She noticed an employee whom she'd seen the week before and she waved at him. He must have remembered seeing her with Rob because he smiled and waved in return. She found the correct hallway and walked into the Housekeeping Manager's office where she had been with Rob the week before. The same 40- something-year-old woman whom she had seen during her visit there with Rob, was still there. "I just tried calling Trevor, but he didn't answer. I've got these girls standing out here, ready to go home, and my day shift girls haven't arrived. What the hell is going on today? This is unacceptable," she yelled.

"Trevor told me that one of the buses broke down. But I'm just here to deliver your invoice for last week's hours," Lucy said.

"Well, tell Trevor I'll expect a huge discount on next week's invoice," she screamed, as she angrily grabbed the invoice from Lucy's hand.

At that point, two agents stepped into the office and flashed their badges. Lucy walked back into the hall and listened as the agents told the woman she was under arrest for knowingly using illegally contracted workers. They then handcuffed her, read her Miranda Rights, and led her out of the office to the parking area where the Sherrif's squad was waiting. The woman glared at Lucy but didn't say a word.

Lucy saw several shy Hispanic girls waiting down a side hallway and recognized Carmen, whom she'd met at the party that started this entire sting. Lucy walked toward the girls. Carmen recognized her and smiled. "I told you I would find a way to help you and the others," Lucy said to her. "People are waiting where you sleep, and they will help you. Don't be afraid."

Carmen just smiled widely at Lucy and then began to explain things to the other girls, as Lucy turned to return to her car.

The two Agents were helping the sheriff's Deputy place the arrested housekeeping manager in the back of their squad car, while she shouted that they had no cause to arrest her because she had no idea what the alleged charges were about.

Looking towards Lucy, the agents simply shook their heads, winked, and gave her a thumbs-up. "Anyone else at this location? If not, where are we heading next, young lady?"

"Follow me, gentlemen," Lucy said and got into her car.

The rest of the deliveries went about the same. The contacts were typically upset that the bus had not delivered their day-shift girls. In one case, there were two people in the office when Lucy entered. One of them bolted out the door as soon as the two agents entered behind her.

Lucy did not recognize the man but assumed he knew what was happening and tried to escape. One of the agents caught up to him and tackled him, then got on his radio to ask the sheriff's Deputy to come inside to assist with these arrests. Lucy wondered if this guy was one of the people organizing the parties where the girls were being sold for sex, and he realized his troubles were greater than those of the housekeeping manager.

Most of those arrested tried to look shocked when they heard the charges being brought against them. But in one instance, the personnel manager said, "I knew this shit was going to fall apart someday." He did not resist arrest.

Some of the people arrested seemed genuinely shocked. It appeared to Lucy that they didn't understand why none of their contract laborers did not speak any English and were being transported to and from work in old church buses. Either they had a convenient naive view of the situation, or they were really that stupid? In either case, Lucy felt that their lack of concern for their employees made them deserve being arrested. *How can people ignore what these girls were living through*, Lucy thought.

Later that evening, Sal and Theresa were waiting for Lucy in the main lobby of her apartment building when she finally made it home.

"I thought I told you that you can go up to my apartment. I think I can trust you both by now," Lucy said.

"Well, this is a special day, Miss Chavez. We are taking you out to dinner while we discuss the final hotel visits for tomorrow. We don't feel that we need to hide our meetings any longer, and in fact, we've invited Rob to be with us. You can go upstairs with Theresa, and she will pack her belongings while you get ready for dinner, so you can have your privacy back."

"I think I'll miss having Tess as a roommate, to be honest. But I guess that life needs to get back to normal sooner or later."

"Well, as normal as it can be with our need to get all the details from you about today, as well as your conversations with Trevor over the last week. Then, of course, the Prosecutors will want to get your statement. Sooner or later, there will be subpoenas for depositions. I wish I could say that you were rid of us, but this may take a while," Sal said. "But for now, you go up with Theresa. I'm going to pick up Rob. I understand that you like Valerio's, so we'll all meet there in about an hour."

Rob was glad to get out of the location where he was being held in protective custody. The two men protecting him had been very friendly, however, they had different interests than

Rob, so Rob found himself spending most of his time reading and surfing the internet. Even then, his protectors didn't allow him to sign on to Facebook or to answer any emails in case a post might alert the Trainor Labor guys that Rob was not actually in jail.

"Did everything go okay at the hotels today?" Rob asked Sal on the drive to Valerio's. Rob nodded in response.

"Great! I was so worried about Lucy. She didn't get hurt at all, did she?"

"Everything went fine, Rob. Lucy carried it off like a pro. And I thought you'd like to hear about this; my Agents saw an old beat-up Lexus following them all morning. They stopped it to question the driver, and it turned out to be my buddy, Burt. He said he was tailing the operation to be sure that Lucy would be okay. We may not have needed his help, but it was nice to see how concerned he was for Lucy's safety."

"I was just so concerned about Lucy being safe," Rob said. "I'm glad that Burt was there to keep an eye on things. I'll be sure to thank him."

"Am I hearing something more than just a casual concern in your voice, Rob?"

"Well, I've tried to keep these feelings under wraps due to the serious nature of this operation, Sal. But I have never felt this attracted to a woman before. I didn't want to say anything to Lucy, in case she didn't have similar feelings for me. It would have made working together very tense."

"I certainly cannot speak for Lucy, but I do know that she has expressed similar concerns for your safety. After tomorrow's work is done, I think you should ask Lucy about her feelings. Having mutual concerns for each other is certainly a good starting point. And just so you know, part of the conversation over dinner is to ask you to accompany Lucy on tomorrow's deliveries. Just in case the word of Trevor's arrest has reached any of those hotels, we thought it may be prudent to have you accompany Lucy to those deliveries."

"Oh, yes! I'd be happy to be involved. I hated being cooped up today, knowing Lucy was going into those hotels alone. And seeing Trevor was the one who made those deliveries that are happening tomorrow, I'm not sure what their reaction may be when Lucy comes in. Those operations are smaller and maybe more paranoid."

"I'm glad you agree," said Sal. "My Agents were just a few steps behind Lucy today, but tomorrow's locations are not as clear-cut. Having you along will divert any negative reactions away from Lucy."

"So, where do you want me to meet up with Lucy?" Rob asked.

"Lucy said she has the invoices for those clients at the Trainor offices. We'll all meet there around 0730. Sound good?" Sal answered.

"I'll be there. I'm glad to see this operation coming to an end."

There were hugs all around when the four met at Valerio's. Rob blushed a lot but seemed to enjoy Lucy's warm greeting. Over dinner, they discussed the day's events and Theresa said that the man who tried to run away at the one hotel was telling all. He had asked for immunity and was willing to testify against everyone else. He was running the sex-for-sale part of the business at that hotel.

"Do you think he may know who was handling that at the other hotels? I don't want to let any of those people escape punishment for what they've done," Lucy asked.

"The agent who interrogated him is hoping that could happen. The man told the agent that some hotels 'shared the sex-girls' if they had a big party and needed more. That part of their operation is well organized. They were getting paid between $350 to $500 per girl at these parties, and even more, if the women stayed all night."

"No wonder Camila heard some of the girls crying when they came back to the barracks. I can't believe that people can treat someone that way," Rob said.

"Well, look at it this way, Rob. Trainor was invoicing around $140,000 per week for the labor, based on what we think is 160 women. That money was declared as income, but the bus services and other expenses reduced their net taxable income. Lucy found only 44 women with those red X's for their

'work time' and that averaged arond twice per week per woman. If they charged just $350 for those 88 times that those women were used, that's over $30,000 a week. That money was not declared and was probably an all-cash business. That money is what those men came to get every second week. There may be others in the Ohio and Buffalo operations, but these four men were probably sharing $60,000 to $100,000 every two weeks. That's a minimum of $7500 of tax-free income per man each week, for selling these enslaved women."

"That's just sick!" Lucy said. "I hope we find all the others. They all need to suffer!"

"Thanks to you and Rob, I think we can guarantee that their bank accounts will be seized, and they will be convicted. These are major criminal charges and they'll be sent away for a long time," Theresa said.

"I saved this one crazy thing until last," Sal said. "One of those men is a retired judge, living in Florida. Greed and disregard for human suffering cuts across all walks of life. You probably thought these men would just be pimps, but the three men we arrested were older, retired businessmen, plus that judge. They could have lived comfortably in retirement, but their greed led them to put this operation together. We'd love to find out how they were able to get these 160 women over the border, but that may not happen. If they squeal on those guys, they have ways to get even with them behind prison bars, not just on the outside."

"So, now we just have one day for the sting portion of this operation. Then, we have the difficult task of interviewing these 160 women. Liz, over in the DA's office, has gathered six Spanish-speaking women to help us. It also appears that Emma and two of the women at the barracks are willing to assist us," Theresa said.

"I assume that Lydia did not want to help?" Rob said.

"Correct," Theresa replied. "When she saw what was happening, she went out to her car and left. Other than not being a compassionate person, it doesn't look like she has done anything illegal." Lucy said, "I'd like to help with interviewing those women."

"What about your job?" Sal asked.

"I'll just ask to extend my vacation. I can't just walk away after all that has happened."

"I'm happy that you offered, and I had wanted to keep you involved. I just didn't want to upset your life any more than we already have. I've already asked my agent in charge, and he said he would be able to justify a temporary, paid position for you as an emergency human services translator. Would you be interested? We think this part of the operation might last six months or longer."

"I'm excited!" Lucy said. "I was so involved, I hated to think about just walking away after this week."

"You would have seen us for quite a while until all the court cases were over, but at least you'll have a way to pay the rent and buy groceries," Theresa said.

After dinner, the four of them were standing in the parking lot of the restaurant, ready to leave. Lucy asked Rob, "Do you want to come by my apartment and pick up Fuzzy? I think he likes me, so I hate to give him back. I can then run you back to your apartment."

Sal interrupted, "Damn. With all the excitement, I don't think that I told my guys to return your belongings to your apartment, Rob. I'll call them now and ask that they do that right away."

Lucy said, "If Rob promises there'll be no 'hanky-panky,' why not have Rob stay at my place tonight? If we need to be at the Trainor office at 7:30 tomorrow, it makes sense."

Rob seemed extremely flustered but said, "You can trust me, Lucy. Really! But it does make sense for tonight."

"A few hugs and a couple kisses are allowed," Lucy said with a big smile on her face. "After all, I need to be sure you want to defend me tomorrow."

Teresa and Sal smiled and gave Lucy a thumbs-up, behind Rob's back.

21

THE SMALL HOTELS

Lucy and Rob showed up early to the Trainor office the following day. The two of them walked in holding hands. Sal and Theresa were in the hallway and smiled broadly,

"Will your agents be there to make the arrests like they did at the other hotels?" Lucy asked Sal and Teresa.

"We're adding another step to the procedure," Sal said. "We'd like you to gather a little more information. We'd like you to wear that wire again today, and at each location, ask for a business card from everyone you meet. If they don't give you a card, at least ask for their name. Then ask some leading questions about how many more employees they may need, and ask 'What type,' to see if they are also expecting to sell their girls for sex. Other than the one small motel, that only has girls for that purpose, I didn't see that any of the invoices for these small hotels included that designation behind any of the employees' names."

"Not this week," Lucy said. "One of the hotels showed one girl with that designation the previous week. And we can't be sure about the weeks before I was there."

"I understand," Rob said. "I assume that I should be the one to ask those questions, seeing Lucy is there for training?"

"You got it," Theresa said. "Lucy could stay involved in the conversations, agreeing with their answers, and so forth. That way they won't become suspicious."

"Okay. Lucy and I will rehearse a little during the drive this morning. I'm sure we can get some good information for you."

"Are we ready to get started?" Lucy asked. "This talk is just making me more nervous."

"One more thing," Sal said. "As you get back to your car after each stop, we want you to talk into the wire so that our agents can hear you. We'd like you to tell us if it is time to go in and make arrests and give us those names, or if we need to hold off at that location. The reason is that we had all of Rob's experience of who was involved with the trafficking at the large, waterfront hotels. But at these outlying, smaller hotels, where Trevor made the deliveries, we don't know the players and what their involvement might be. For example, if the only person you meet at a hotel is just an uninformed clerical worker who takes the invoice, we may not blow your cover today. We still plan to stop the deliveries of the girls the next day, so the upset phone calls to Trainor, received tomorrow, will give us the information we need to pay them another visit and make any arrests."

"That sounds like a good plan," Lucy said. "I'm sure that between Rob and myself, we can help to make those decisions for you."

"Okay, then. I think you're ready to go. My agents will get as close to each hotel as possible, without raising suspicion. If at any time you feel threatened, just say so, and my guys will rush in, Sal said."

Lucy and Rob rehearsed a few scenarios they could use during their meetings with people in the hotels. Their first stop was at a larger chain hotel near Kearsarge.

Rob and Lucy entered through the rear service entrance and a large Black man, dressed in a custodian's uniform, saw them enter. "I'm sorry folks," the man said. "Guests need to use the front entrance."

Rob answered, "Actually, we're here to meet with the manager or whoever deals with the contracted laundry and cleaning staff."

"Do you work with that guy, Trevor? He usually comes out every couple of weeks and I've seen him go into Pricilla's office. Do you know where that is?"

"No, we don't. Trevor has changed jobs, and this is only Lucy's second time out here. Could you direct us there? My name's Rob, and this is Lucy."

"Sure, follow me. I'll take you there. My name is Maxwell. I'm the Maintenance Manager. Can I mention that these four girls in the laundry are real workaholics? We love them. I wish we could find local women that worked that hard. I think Priscilla is also thinking about replacing some of our maids with Trevor's girls."

"I thought these were local women," Lucy said.

"I'm not stupid," Maxwell said. "Not one of these girls can speak more than a few words of English, and if I talk to them, they act like my neighbor's abused dogs. They're afraid to look me in the eye and they stay away from everyone other than themselves. I know they must all be illegals, but that's none of my business. They're great workers and we try to treat them right."

"I had no idea. Thanks, Maxwell."

Maxwell led Lucy and Rob past the laundry, where he waved at two Hispanic girls. They smiled and waved back. "There's a couple of the girls," Maxwell said. "That one girl looks like she's not more than sixteen, but the older one, Marga, keeps an eye on her like a mother hen. We've been giving her food to take home with them."

They made a turn down another hallway and Maxwell continued, "I can tell that they don't eat well, so I've been setting aside the leftovers from our free breakfast buffet for them. Seeing they're scared to talk to me, I just set the bag in their locker, where they keep their jackets when they're working. I see them eating it when they take a break, so I hope it helps them."

"That's very thoughtful of you, Maxwell. I'll be sure to look into what they're being fed," Lucy said. "They can't do a good day's work if the girls come in hungry."

"My wife sent me to work last winter with some old, but warm jackets for them. I could tell that they were not dressed warm enough for our winters. But the girls seemed frightened to take them. What's that all about? I tried to talk with Trevor about that, but he just ignored me."

"You're a good man, Maxwell. Thank you for telling us. We'll be doing something about these issues. Trust me."

"I sure hope so," Maxwell said. "I don't care whether these girls are illegals or not, I just want to see them treated right."

"I'll let you know, once we've handled it," Lucy said.

"Well, here is Priscilla's office. Please don't tell her what I told you. I don't think she gives a shit about the girls. She just likes that they work so cheap."

"Your information is just between us," Rob said. "By the way, have you seen any signs of the girls being abused, either physically or sexually?"

"Not that I'm aware of," Maxwell said. "If I'd seen that happening, I'd have called the cops. Even Priscilla hasn't allowed that to happen."

"Glad to hear that. Thanks for your concern and kindness, Maxwell."

Rob knocked and then led the way into Priscilla's office. The sign on her door said, Priscilla Monroe, General Manager. Priscilla was a stern-looking woman, about 45 years old, dressed in a Navy-Blue pants suit.

"Can I help you?" Priscilla asked as soon as they entered. "If you have a guest room issue, please let the Reception Desk Clerk know."

"We're here from Trainor Labor to deliver the invoice. Trevor has changed jobs and Lucy is in training. My name is Rob. I've been with Trainor for about a year, and I handle the waterfront hotels." "So, Trevor won't be handling things anymore? He and I had some agreements that I'd hate to lose, seeing you guys are my new contacts."

"What kind of deals Miss Monroe? I can probably work with you," Lucy said.

"Well, the owner only wants to pay for four girls, but occasionally I need five or six when we have a big conference in town. Trevor would send me a couple more at a reduced rate and I just paid him cash."

"We can maybe work that out," Lucy said.

Priscilla just smiled at Lucy's response, which was the only smile she gave during the entire visit. Then Priscilla said, "But I am busy, so just give me the invoice and I need to get back to my emails."

Rob handed the invoice to Priscilla, and they turned and walked out with nothing more said.

"So, if you guys heard all of that, I think we could hold off on any arrests here today, Lucy said once they got to the car. I think we might want to learn what the hotel owner knows, seeing he seems to be the one concerned with keeping the cost down. It also sounds like Trevor had some side deals going, and I'm sure that those cash payments went into his pocket. But it didn't sound like she wanted those girls for anything more than extra labor."

"I agree, Lucy. And let's remember to come out here and take Maxwell and his wife out for a nice dinner, once the dust settles. It's great to know that there are still some great, caring people like him around," Rob said.

"When the girls don't show up tomorrow morning, I'm sure Priscilla will be on the phone to Trainor. Maybe there would be a way to get the owner involved when that happens."

"Yes. I'd have liked to tell Maxwell what was happening, but it's too early for that. Where do we head next, Rob?"

"We've got another small chain hotel in Meadville. I think that's on our way over to those hotels near the New York border."

The Meadville hotel started the same way as the one in Kearsarge. The only difference was that instead of being met by a nice man like Maxwell, they encountered an older woman screaming at one of the maids outside the laundry. The maid was young and Hispanic, and certainly one of Trainor's employees. She was standing with her arms across her chest and her head bowed, looking down at the floor.

The older woman was yelling in a mixture of English and Spanish, which Lucy loosely understood as, "I'll be sure Trevor sends your lazy Mexican ass back to Guadalajara, or whatever hellhole you came from. What the hell happened to you last night? Your ass is dragging this morning."

"Ma'am, can I interrupt?" Rob said, interrupting the woman's tirade. "We're here in place of Trevor, can we help you?"

"I want to talk to Trevor. I never want to see this Mexican bitch again," the older woman said.

While Rob was talking to the woman, Lucy took the maid aside and whispered that she should go back to work. Lucy told her that things would change by that evening. The maid looked at Lucy and told her that the girls who had returned from the waterfront hotels had said things were going to change, so when she was taken to work this morning, she was very upset and refused to work. Lucy asked her to go and tell the other girls to just finish up their work for the day and that they would not be coming back to work the next day. Lucy smiled just thinking of the joy the other girls were going to feel when they heard the news.

Rob had calmed the woman down a little. Through their interaction, he had discovered that she was the head housekeeper.

"I'm taking you to the Manager's office," the woman said to Lucy and Rob. "The Manager called the owner because this was the day that Trevor said he was coming. He and his wife are here, and they are ready to bite Trevor's head off. This bullshit needs to stop. These illegal bitches had better do what I tell them, or there will be hell to pay."

As soon as Lucy and Rob entered the Manager's office, the Head Housekeeper told the three people in the office, "Mr. Carvelli, I don't like what is going on here today. Apparently, Trevor sent these two young punks out here instead of coming here himself. I told that lazy one that I'd have her ass sent back to Mexico for refusing to work. I don't know what's going on, but I'm not going back to cleaning toilets and making beds. So, they'd better solve this nightmare. I understand that there is also a work slowdown in the laundry this morning."

The owner and his wife tried to appease the complaining woman and assured her that they would get to the bottom of what was going on within the organization. Something had gone wrong somewhere, and they were going to do everything in their power to get to the bottom of it.

Turning to Rob, the owner asked who he and Lucy were and what roles they played in his organization.

"My name is Rob, and this is Lucy. Trevor has moved away, so we were sent to deliver the latest invoice."

"Well, my wife Melinda and I own the franchise on three hotels, and Trevor supplies the workers for all of them. Margaret Seavers here called us this morning about this slowdown, which looks like some type of strike. I don't know how a bunch of illegal Hispanic girls think that they can make demands. They're lucky to be in the United States with a place to sleep and food to eat. Are you speaking on Trevor's behalf? If not, I want to talk with one of your supervisors."

Rob looked at Lucy and smiled. "Actually, there are some people close behind us who would like to speak with you. Lucy, if you would keep these nice people occupied, I'll go out back and see where our friends might be. Excuse me, but I'll be right back."

Rob went back to the rear service entrance just as the car of FBI agents pulled in.

"We heard your conversation, Rob. I think those four have buried themselves sufficiently already, so it's time we read them their rights and take them downtown."

Lucy kept the conversation going and was able to determine the names of the other two hotels owned by Mr. Corvelli. That would make those stops quicker today, just to see the involvement of the Manager and Head Housekeeper.

Rob re-entered the office with the two agents. "Would you like me to introduce you, or would you like to do the honors?" Rob asked the agents.

Mr. Corvelli interrupted, "I hope you guys are prepared to put a stop to this shitstorm. This is screwing up my business."

The senior agent looked to Rob and said, "I guess that legally, I had better take over. I am addressing this to all four of you in this room. 'You have the right to remain silent. Anything you do say can be ......"

"What's this shit?" Corvelli said.

"I'll let Agent Lester finish reading your rights, but the four of you are under arrest, under the suspicion of knowingly using undocumented workers in your business," said the second agent.

"How would we know that they were illegals?" Corvelli bellowed.

"I think you should just listen to the rest of your rights."

The next hotel they visited also happened to have two employees who were used for sex parties like the one Lucy had stumbled across at the Fiesta Bay Hotel. The event that had set this sting operation in motion.

Lucy wanted to begin this sting by getting those girls out first. Rob agreed that was a great idea, so Lucy called Theresa and asked her to check the phone photos of the timecards. "I always photographed the timecards that had the red x's on them," Lucy said. Theresa dug through the photos and when she found them, she confirmed Rob and Lucy's location.

"You're at the Countryside Inn, right?"

"Yes, that's it. Do you see the two with red x's?"

"I see Alicia and Sofia. Does that sound correct?"

"Yes, that's the two I remembered. They had been used both weeks, two times per week. Do you think we can just ask the hotel manager to see them? And then can we get a transport out here to take them back to the rest of the girls?"

"Of course," Theresa said. "Try to find out if the manager or someone else is responsible for selling them for sex. I'll get transport going to take all six girls from that hotel, and I'll tell the Agents to expect at least one arrest at that location."

Rob led the way into the hotel and found the laundry. Two Hispanic girls were working there with a middle-aged woman who appeared to be the Head Housekeeper. When asked, the housekeeper directed them to the front desk and told them to ask for Gabriel, the hotel manager.

The desk clerk called Gabriel from her phone and a flashy man with an attitude appeared. He was over-dressed for a manager in this type of hotel and when Rob told him they had come to deliver the Trainor invoice, he snapped back, "Where the hell is Trevor? He promised me some younger girls this week. I hope she isn't what he promised!" as he pointed at Lucy.

"Hardly," Rob snapped back. Rob showed that he didn't appreciate the comment directed at Lucy. "And would you please call Alicia and Sofia to the office?"

"No. I'm keeping those two. They're fine. I want the other two housekeepers replaced. They're not lookers like Ally & Sofia. I need all four to be of the quality needed for our parties. You mean that Trevor is reneging on our deal?"

"I think you should call all four of the housekeepers down here," Lucy said. "It appears that you aren't happy, and we have a way to satisfy you, I think."

"Who the hell do you think you are, you Mexican bitch? You don't give me orders." With that, Rob had heard enough and he back-handed Gabriel across the face. He had apparently broken his nose, because blood gushed out.

Gabriel started screaming and the Desk Clerk ran in. When she saw Gabriel holding his face, with all the blood pouring out, she asked, "Did you do that?"

Rob sheepishly nodded his head yes, wondering if he had overreacted.

The Desk Clerk, a girl in her late twenties, then asked, "Is this because of how he treats those girls?"

Lucy answered, "Yes. How much do you know about it?"

"I know it all. If Gabriel won't be around to retaliate, I'd love to tell you anything you want to know."

Gabriel gurgled through his bloody nose, "Keep your mouth shut, Tony."

Lucy said, "Don't worry, Tony. The FBI is outside, ready to take him into custody. Can you get all six of the contracted girls down here for us? We're taking them with us, and then I'm sure the Agents will love to arrange for you to provide a statement."

When Tony, the desk clerk, left to find the girls, Rob whispered into the microphone hidden in the hair behind Lucy's left ear, "Theresa, I hope I didn't get anyone in trouble, but he deserved that."

Lucy then turned to Rob, kissing him gently on the mouth, and said, "Very gallant. Thank you for defending me."

Just then, the two Agents entered the hotel lobby and called Lucy's name.

"In here, behind the desk," Lucy yelled.

When the Agents walked in and saw the blood, which had finally stopped gushing from Gabriel's nose, they both broke into a smile. As one Agent read Gabriel his rights, the other gave Rob a "thumbs-up" sign from behind Gabriel's back.

Gabriel asked, "And how do I file charges for being assaulted by an FBI Agent?"

"You weren't assaulted by any agents. This guy isn't an FBI Agent. He's with your contractor." As they led Gabriel out of the hotel, he looked thoroughly confused.

Next, the desk clerk came to the lobby with six young women, all looking very bewildered. "I think you asked about Alicia and Sofia. This is Alicia and this is Sofia. Then I know this lady as Matty and this one as Josie, who are also housekeepers. The last two are Juana and Catalina, who work in the laundry. Do I understand that you are taking them with you?"

"Yes," the Agent said. "These women were being used here illegally. I hope you understand."

"I certainly understand and I'm so happy that they are being rescued. Gabriel was misusing them all, but particularly Alicia and Sofia. He tried to keep me in the dark about what he was doing, but when guests started asking me, 'How do I order one of those girls,' I started to figure it out. When I complained to Gabriel, he told me to keep my mouth shut or he'd have Trevor silence me. I'd seen Trevor meeting with Gabriel, and I was afraid, so I didn't know what to do."

Rob then asked, "What about the hotel owners, Tony? Are they aware of what Gabriel was doing?

"I really don't think so, sir. They live in Arizona, and they only visit the hotel a few times a year. As long as they were seeing a monthly return on their investment, they had left the operating details to Gabriel. When Gabriel found this contractor who could supply labor at half of what we were paying our local housekeepers, he jumped at the chance. I'm not sure, but I suspect that he pocketed the savings.

"Somewhere along the way, I think Trevor suggested the idea of selling the girls to those guys. I saw the changes in Alicia's and Sofia's attitude towards me and the Head Housekeeper. It was always strained, but it then became fearful, particularly when Gabriel was around. They no longer smiled, and they even avoided looking at us. I knew a girl in my high school who was being abused, and I remembered similar reactions from her when the abuse began. That's when I confronted Gabriel, and he reacted with what I took to be that threat about Trevor silencing me."

"Tony, I'm sure the FBI will want to interview you further. Are you willing to cooperate?"

"Of course," Tony replied. "Here's my cell phone number. As long as I'm still working here, you can also reach me here. I guess I will need to call the owners and tell them what happened, so I don't know what they will say. I'll need to tell them that we need to hire new people for housekeeping and laundry."

"I think we'd like to have one of our Agents listening to that phone call," the Agent said. "I'm sure you must understand that we'd like to hear the reactions from the owners."

"I certainly understand that," Tony said. "And by the way, my full name is Tonia, but everyone calls me Tony."

"Well, Tonia. I appreciate your cooperation. Thank you," said the Agent.

The Agent went back into the Manager's Office with Tony to make the call to the hotel owners, and the van transported the six women back to the barracks. Rob and Lucy then left to finish the rest of their deliveries.

The stings at the rest of the hotels were not as dramatic as they were at the last two. The manager at one of the hotels was arrested, and two others at two other hotels were told they would be brought in for questioning once the investigation started.

Rob had held the small motel as the last stop of the day. It was where the girls suspected of only being used as prostitutes were being held. Lucy told the Agents through her wire, who were following close behind them driving up to the motel, that they should expect to make an arrest, but to wait as long as they could before entering the motel ''s office. Lucy entered the office and Rob was a few feet behind. Rex saw Lucy and said, "So, did Trev send you back alone? Maybe I can talk you into staying."

Rob heard Rex's statement as he walked through the door and said, "I don't think this lady is in the same league as your staff. How many tricks per week do you sell them? I'm curious."

Thinking that Rob was serious, Rex said, "At least twice per night. They complain if I try to get them more than two. The guys are complaining. I need a couple more lookers. I've told Trev that for several weeks now."

"Do you think we need any more, Lucy?" Should we call them?" Rob asked.

"So, you did bring me more girls, then," Rex said, having misunderstood Rob's question.

"No. We have another surprise for you," Lucy said. "You can come in now, fellas."

The two agents walked into the motel office and began to read Rex his rights. Lucy was amazed to see that Rex was completely speechless, and he walked out to the parking lot and peacefully entered ' car.

"That's not at all what I expected," Lucy said. She then grabbed Rob, hugged him, and relaxed into his arms. "I think we've worked ourselves out of a job, my man. I don't know if we should celebrate or what.

At that moment, Lucy's cell phone rang. She saw it was Teresa. "Hi, Tess. What now?"

"Sal and I just realized that with Rex arrested, we've left a motel with five unemployed prostitutes and a bunch of guests, for lack of a better term, with nobody watching the store. Can you talk to the girls out there, explain what happened, and we will send a bust to transport them. We are still discussing what to do with those girls, because we don't want to take them to the factory with the others."

"Wow! We've created a real predicament, didn't we?" Lucy said.

"I guess it had to be done, but we just never saw this problem coming. The other hotels had staff to allow them to limp along until they found more employees. With Rex arrested and those five girls out of a job, that place may need to be closed," Sal said into Teresa's phone. "I've put in a call to my

Agent in Charge, because I've never been faced with a situation like this."

"Maybe you can arrest all the guys who have been paying for these girls," Rob said into Lucy's phone.

"In the State of New York, their laws actually say that the men who pay for sex are breaking the law, but in Pennsylvania, they just get their hand slapped and names recorded."

"Seeing we will be waiting here for your bus to show up, should we tell the guests they are no longer welcome?" Rob asked.

"If there are any there, I think you can do that. I assume the working guys may not be there," Sal said. "I think we may be sending a Deputy Sherriff out there to close the place down. So, if you two don't mind, keep an eye on the place until the bus and the Deputy Sherrif arrive. And Lucy, please explain what happened to those girls. And thanks to both of you for handling this very tough day so professionally."

Lucy saw one of the girls outside hanging laundry, like she had noticed the previous week. She went out through the back door of the office and greeted her. The woman did not appear surprised, probably thinking that Rex had found another girl to work with them. When Lucy began explaining the situation to her, she was surprised to see the woman begin to cry. She asked her why she was crying.

"I don't want to go home," the woman said in Spanish. "Here we have enough to eat, a clean place to sleep, and we can complain to Rex. At home, I will die."

Lucy tried to console the woman, but she started to realize just how hard life must be for these women in Central America, where their families have thrown them out and they live on the streets, selling their bodies just to survive.

On the day of the sting, the Trainor-owned bus drivers arrived at the factory that served as the barracks for the workers and were arrested and read their rights as soon as they stepped out of their buses. The agents later said that the drivers all said that they expected this would happen sooner or later. Then, when the drivers were being interrogated, they all admitted that they understood this was some sort of illegal operation. They knew that having all these Latina girls living in an old, dirty factory had to be illegal, but they all felt they would be in big trouble if they said anything or tried to report it to the authorities. Other than Rob's conscience, it seemed like all of the locals who saw what was happening just turned a blind eye to the situation. One of the old church buses was driven by a younger man who refused to talk.

During the confusion that followed, that driver bolted from the bus and ran into the hotel service entrance. An agent ordered the driver to stop, but he was inside the hotel before the agent could follow him. It was later determined that he was the Trainor employee who ran the bus transport part of the business. A warrant was issued for the driver's arrest, and he was apprehended several days later while trying to break into the Trainor offices. It was assumed that he was trying to find and destroy any documents linking him to the business.

The hotel buses received the same treatment as the hotel staff, and surprisingly, those drivers seemed relieved to see that this "fiasco," as one man called it, was finally over. Not one of the drivers thought this was normal, or legal, yet none of them reported the situation.

Beth, Liz's friend at the Erie Women's Rescue Center, had contacted local food pantries and other charities to obtain food and clothing for the rescued women. She also contacted the local University to find Spanish-speaking women who would be willing to work with the INS to determine how each woman would be processed.

Once Rob and Lucy completed their invoice deliveries to those last hotels, Rob figured that he was done with the operation and that he was out of work. He found Sal Dominico and stuck out his hand. When Sal shook Rob's hand, Rob began, "It was nice working with you and Theresa, Sal. I hope to see you..."

Sal quickly interrupted, saying, "Do you have something lined up, Rob? If not, please don't run away. We really could use your help around here. You know more about the good and bad around here than anyone. You could be a huge help."

"I can assist as much as I can, Sal. But I need to find a job. I have bills to pay."

"I'm not promising a huge salary or long-term employment, Rob. But I've convinced my Agent in Charge that your services would save me at least two more Agents being used during this part of the investigation. You know the people involved at the large hotels, you know about how these barracks were operated, including the food supply, and you are friends with Camila. She seems a little shaken by all that happened, so first of all, I'd appreciate your help to calm her down and explain what happened. Tell her about your cooperation with the FBI and how Lucy was involved. With that information coming from you, I need Camila to stay here, with pay, until we can place all these women in other facilities."

"That sounds great, Sal. But please warn me before you need to cut me loose so that I can start looking for a job."

"I've given that some thought as well," Sal said. "I know you had started in college. After this glimpse into what we do in the FBI, do you think you might consider it as a career?"

"Well sure, Sal. But I'm two years away from my degree."

"With an agreement to work with the FBI for a minimum of time spent in college, plus working for us as an Intern, I can get you a scholarship at the university here in Erie. How does that sound?" "You can do that? It sounds wonderful," Rob answered.

"The government offers scholarships to promising prospects all the time. Several of the Agents working on this investigation started that way. I did have one graduate who left the FBI after fulfilling their required time, so this would not have to be a lifelong commitment."

"I must admit that I've been very impressed by what I've witnessed this past week. Not to mention that it allowed me to meet and work with Lucy. But if this is a serious offer, then I am very interested."

"I've already run background checks on you, and you've passed those with flying colors. So, please do not look for other employment. I will get the paperwork started once things calm down around here. But for now, please work with Lucy and Liz, and please talk with Camila. We really need her help."

"Sal, I can't thank you enough. Two weeks ago, I was upset and ready to get away from Trainor. Now, because of Trainor, I have met Lucy, met you, and have a promising career in my future. Amazing how just ten days can change your entire life, and in my case, positively."

22

KISHI'S STORY

Lucy wanted to meet and hear the stories of the first group of rescued women who came into the Family Shelter. She was happy to tag along with Liz, who also wanted to talk to the ladies, but did not speak Spanish. Lucy was glad to be playing the role of translator.

Lucy was curious to know how the two Native girls ended up amongst this group of mostly Hispanic women, so she sought out Kishi and Yellowbird. She found out that Yellowbird was the nickname for Judy Jackson, from South Dakota. She asked about Judy, but the Center's staff said she was sleeping. As she was talking to the staff, she saw Kishi and made eye contact with her. Kishi smiled and walked over to where Lucy and Liz were standing. She stood a little away from them until Lucy finished talking and then came forward. Kishi said, "Can I hug you, Miss Chavez? I've heard about what you did to help bring these animals to justice. I can't thank you enough!"

Lucy hugged Kishi. "Please call me Lucy," she said. "I know your first name is Kishi, but don't know your last name.

I had a classmate in high school named Kishi, so I know you must have a Native American background."

"Yes, Kishi was the name my mom gave me, but in school, they called me Julia Stone. Was your high school classmate a Native? Some Anglo girls are being named with our names down here, but that doesn't happen up in Canada."

"Yes, she was from here in Erie. She was from a small town nearby. Her parents had lived on a nearby Ohio reservation. They moved to Erie so that Kishi could attend a better school."

Lucy was curious to know how Kishi had ended up in this situation. She was a very pretty Native girl, but at 24 years old, she did not fit the picture of the young runaways Lucy had heard about. First, Lucy introduced her to Liz and explained that Liz and Burt were the real source of the rescue effort. But then Lucy decided to ask her, "Kishi, how did you end up here?"

"I was up on the rez near Apitipi. I had finished high school but had no real opportunities for a good job. Canada makes public apologies for how we were treated, with Indigenous Day events and so on, but the average Canadian either ignores us or just wishes we'd disappear. We aren't mistreated, like back in my grandparents' days, but I was getting frustrated by being turned down for good jobs, or being told that I wasn't qualified."

"Just so I follow you, Kishi, by rez, you mean reservation? Were you living on a reservation in Canada?"

"It was in a residential area adjacent to the actual reservation; mostly small, rundown houses, lots of bars, and a bunch of trailer parks. I would catch a ride into town and hang out with a bunch of young Anglo girls at the mall. I was hoping that something would rub off on me, I guess. However, I'm not sure that the opportunities available to them could ever rub off on someone who looked like me. But the girls were friendly and seemed to accept my friendship, so I enjoyed my time with them," Kishi answered.

"Ahh, I see. So, you started hanging out at the mall quite regularly? How did that lead to getting you down here?"

"One of the girls was from Toronto. She was a little older than the others, and she seemed to have a good job down there. At least she always had more money than the rest of the group, and she'd buy us pizza. She seemed to take a liking to me, and when she found out that I was 21, she asked me to have a drink with her. The other girls were underage, so it was her way of getting me alone, I now realize. We sat in the bar that night and she started complimenting me, telling me how pretty I was, and that I had some class. She asked why I didn't have a good job because I told her I was just making coffee at Horton's."

"I see it coming, I guess," Liz broke in. "I have worked most of my career against traffickers, and they usually start by handing out compliments. But it was probably easy for that girl, Kishi, because you really are beautiful."

"Well, thanks, Liz. I never felt beautiful back home, but once down here, I think my looks worked against me."

"I understand," Liz said. "But please continue with your story."

"After that night, this woman asked me to meet her at a bar away from the mall. I see now that she didn't want those younger girls to hear our conversations. She said that she had talked to her boss in Toronto, and she had recommended me for a hospitality job opening in the United States. I told her that I didn't have a passport to travel across the border, and the woman told me that her boss could take care of that."

"That didn't raise a red flag for you?" Liz asked.

"I guess it should have, but the chance for a hospitality job, which I thought would be as a reception desk clerk or concierge in a nice hotel, had me seeing my way out of the rez, once and for all. This woman was good at her job, and she had me hooked. She said that if I was interested, she was heading back to Toronto the next morning. I didn't want to tell my mom because she might want to check everything out, so I agreed to stay with her at her hotel that night."

"She really worked fast," Lucy said. "So, how long was that from that first meeting at the mall?"

"It was just three days from the first meeting until that night. I told her I didn't want to leave my clothes and other things behind, but she said I could get those when I came home to visit. She said she'd let me wear her clothes until I could get some in the United States. And then that night in the hotel, we slept in the same bed, and I was a bit shocked that she wanted us to sleep naked. She started caressing and kissing me, and I must admit that I enjoyed her attention. Now, I think she was just testing me, to see if I would object to sexual advances."

"That woman, Lorain, you called her, was a real pro! She is probably a full-time recruiter for a trafficking organization. Most young girls are kidnapped by traffickers, who are usually young women befriending the young kids on the beach or in malls. Some of your friends at the mall may have eventually been kidnapped by her. Those who get kidnapped are probably drugged when the trafficker's girl offers to drive them home or just offers them a drink in their car while at the beach. In your case, she knew you wanted a good job, so she didn't need to use drugs or kidnap you against your will."

"I see that now. And I guess it helped her that I enjoyed her intimate attention that night. When we got to Toronto the next day, she introduced me to a man that she said was her boss. Now, I can see that he probably wasn't the boss, but a young, great-looking guy who smiled and talked nicely to me. After the meeting, Lorain said I could seal the deal by sleeping with the boss. I think she saw the fear on my face, so she said, 'He's really sweet. I have spent the night with him occasionally. He's gentle and he'll wear a condom.'"

"Oh my! I'm shocked that they took that chance to scare you off," said Lucy.

"That night I spent with Lorain, she had asked me if I was a virgin, and I told her that I'd been active with a boy in high school. I guess she figured that I would agree, and I did. The man was gentle, treated me with respect, and thinking that he was responsible for getting this job for me, I tried to be receptive to him."

"How long before they got you over the border? You didn't have a passport, right? Liz asked.

"The next morning, Lorain took me to a warehouse outside of Toronto. She said there was a hold-up on my passport, but the hotel in the United States wanted me on the job as soon as possible. They showed me a secret compartment in the baggage compartment of a bus, which had been padded with foam rubber. The driver said I could ride with him on the bus until we got to the loading point near Niagara, but then I'd hide in that compartment before they loaded the passengers' luggage. They gave me several bottles of water and a blanket, warning me not to drink too much, because I'd have to pee in the compartment."

"And what did you think at that point, Kishi? You must have started to see that something was wrong."

"I weakly objected to being in that compartment. It was ventilated somehow, but I had very little room to even turn. But looking back, I guess I still believed that this was going to result in a good job in the States, so I did what Lorain said. You have to realize how fed-up I was with my life back home. I was in that compartment for not even an hour when I heard them load passengers on the bus. I think I fell asleep because the next I knew the passengers were getting off the bus and the bus pulled away. About ten minutes later, the bus stopped again, and someone opened the compartment. They took me to that place where your team found me a couple days ago."

Liz said, "I think Lorain had drugged those bottles of water she gave you, Kishi. They didn't want to take a chance that you might freak out in that compartment and start screaming. In a way, I'm glad she did that, so you weren't in fear during that whole trip. I don't like cramped spaces, so I would have freaked out."

"I never thought of that," Kishi said. "I know that they took the other two bottles away when I got to the arrival location. I have no idea how long I was in that compartment, but I never even finished that first bottle."

"Yup. It had to be drugged. I'm assuming they drove in at Niagara Falls. That's a busy border crossing, so they probably are not looking closely at the luggage compartments. I'm sure the FBI will warn them to pay closer attention to those buses," Liz said. "What did the house mothers at that old house tell you when you first arrived?" Liz continued.

"House mothers? What do you mean? Kishi asked.

"Oh, sorry. That's what we call those older women who work for the traffickers. It's their job to keep you there and report any problems to the traffickers. Were they friendly or did they act like jailers?"

"There were a couple of nasty ones, but the other four were sorta friendly. They all spoke Spanish to the other girls, but they seemed to understand that Yellowbird and I were different. I asked one of them when I would get my Passport and she told me, *'You're here now. You don't need a passport anymore'* And when I said that I'd want to go home on my vacation time, the lady smiled and said, *'That won't happen for a long time, young lady.'*"

"Oh my, did the lightbulb come on at that point?" Lucy asked Kishi.

"I was hoping that the woman didn't know what she was saying, but I did start to get worried. The next morning, they woke us up early and I was handed a uniform that said 'Fiesta Bay Hotel' over my right chest and 'Staff Cleaner' over my left chest. I told the lady that you called the housemother that there had to be some mistake because I was there for a hospitality job. She laughed a little and said, 'That will come later.'"

"Was your thinking starting to change at that point?" Liz asked.

"I was certainly worried, but still hopeful. Lorain and her boss had promised me that job, so maybe there was just a mistake. I certainly didn't realize that I'd been lied to and kidnapped, even though I had agreed to what got me here. Now I realize how naive I was to have believed them."

"Don't feel too bad, Kishi. You weren't the first and I'm sure others will believe those good recruiters, like Lorain. This was not some amateur operation, and you were lied to by some well-trained operators. I'm sure that our FBI guys will want to hear all the details in order to get the Canadian investigators to track down Lorain and the others up in Canada. Are you willing to help them?"

"I'd love to see Lorain and the others go to jail. I hope they didn't kidnap those other girls I'd befriended in the Black River Mall, which is just a strip mall. I was naïve, but those girls knew nothing about life. I survived the drunken guys they made me have sex with, but I'm not sure that some of those girls would survive. I hated what the bosses here were making me do, but I heard some of the Latina girls talking about some girl who promised to help, and I knew that I just had to hold on until help came."

Liz laughed. "I'm sure you don't know this, Kishi, but the girl who promised to help is sitting right here." Liz pointed at Lucy.

"Oh my God, Lucy! Really? That was you?"

"About a month ago, I thought I was on a date. The guy I was with took me to his room, where I saw three Hispanic girls. I talked to one of them in the restroom and heard what was happening to them. I promised to help, and a asked a friend for help, and he introduced me to Liz. And here we are. Was the girl's name Carmen who you heard talking?"

"Yes, it was Carmen. I haven't seen her here. I hope she's okay. I know she hated those sex parties."

Liz put up a hand to stop Kishi. "Before we continue with your story, I think we should get one of the investigators in here," Liz said to Kishi. "What happened once you started working at the hotel is part of their investigation. But I will also want you to repeat this story about what happened in Canada so that the Canadian authorities can be notified."

Kishi and Lucy nodded in agreement.

23

CARMEN

Lucy asked Liz if they could find Carmen and talk with her. Lucy still felt a connection to Carmen because of their chance meeting at that party. After all, that conversation is what had started this entire investigation and rescue.

Liz asked the INS team manager if they had met a girl named Carmen. She was surprised to hear that they had interviewed three young women, all named Carmen. Apparently, Carmen was a common name in Latin America. Liz thought it would be interesting to speak with all three of the girls the INS team had interviewed, but it turned out that one of those women had been at the small motel and was determined to be a professional prostitute. That woman asked to return to her village in Guatemala.

The two remaining *Carmens* were asked to come to one of the small conference rooms that had been set up on the main floor of the Barracks. Lucy immediately recognized Carmen, the one she had met weeks before at the Fiesta Bay Hotel. Carmen ran up to Lucy and hugged her tightly.

"You didn't forget about us!" Carmen said, with tears falling down her cheeks.

Lucy explained to Liz what Carmen had just said, and why she was crying. Liz nodded solemnly. Then, turning back to Carmen, Lucy said in Spanish, "Of course not! I told you that I would find a way to help."

Lucy asked Carmen to introduce the other girl.

"Carmen is from Nicaragua," Carmen said to Lucy, "and because we shared the same name, we have become friends. I told Carmen about meeting you at the hotel and told her that I was waiting for you to find a way to help us. Carmen and I worked at different hotels, but we stayed very close here in this prison."

Liz was shocked to hear Carmen refer to the Barracks as a prison, so she asked Lucy to have Carmen describe how they got to the barracks and what their life was like once they got to Erie.

"You may remember that I had come from Guatemala," Carmen began telling her story to Liz, Lucy, and the INS team manager. She spoke in Spanish and Lucy acted as her translator.

"My family was poor, and I would find small jobs to help bring money to my mother. When I was sixteen, I met a young man who told me that he could get me a good job in the United States, and I could send money home to my mother. He said that if I could give him 150 Quetzal, that's about twenty dollars, he would arrange the job for me. I asked my mother, and she said it sounded good, so she borrowed the money from neighbors, and I met the man the next day. That night, I joined about twenty other women on a bus, and we drove into Mexico. We were on the bus for at least two days. They only fed us bread and bananas, and very little water. We asked for more water, but the men on the bus said they didn't want us stopping to take pees. When we complained, the men just laughed at us."

"My God, Carmen! Did you then realize this was not a good thing to be doing?"

"All of us wanted those jobs in the United States, so we were used to a hard life, and we thought this was a way to find something better," Carmen said.

"So, what happened when you got to Mexico?" Lucy asked.

"The bus stopped at a small fishing village, and we got on a boat. Then they had us crawl into a big place that smelled like fish. One of the girls found some dead fish behind a piece of steel and two of the girls ate them. A while later, both of those girls got sick. But once the boat started sailing, we were rolling a lot, and most of us got very dizzy and eventually became sick. After about three hours, we were told to come out of that big hole. It was so good to breathe clean air again.

"We saw three small fishing boats next to us and they divided us up into the three boats. The men on those boats started arguing, saying that they wanted one of the girls because she was a pretty one. One man said he wasn't getting what he had paid for, so he grabbed that girl and pushed her onto his boat. The men on the three boats told the young man that I knew that we all looked sick, so he hadn't fed us enough to deliver healthy ones. I saw the young man I met in Guatemala take a lot of Mexican Pesos from the three men on the small boats, and then the big fishing boat left. I was with seven other girls. We were back in another big place that smelled like fish. We saw dead fish laying inside, but didn't want to eat them in case they made us sick."

"That must have been terrible," Liz said.

"At least we were only on this boat a few hours," Carmen said. "And the men on that boat gave us bread with some meat inside, and they also gave us several pails of fresh water. They told us to use one of the empty pails for our pee.

"When it was dark, the men brought us out of the big hole and asked us if we could swim. I had been swimming in the river near my home, but never in the ocean. Only one girl said that she was a good swimmer. The men then pointed out towards the water and asked if we could see the three bright lights on the shore. They gave each one of us a big piece of wood and told us to jump over the side and swim to those lights. We were all afraid, even the girl who said she was a good swimmer. We did what we were told, but there were some big waves when we got close to the shore and one of the girls slipped off her board. We never saw her again."

"This is just terrible, what these girls went through just to get here," Liz said to Lucy. "What happened then?"

Lucy asked Carmen Liz's question and Carmen continued, "We told the men on shore that one of the girls had slipped off her board, but they just ignored us and split us into three different cars.

Again, they were arguing over who would take the prettiest girls, which we didn't understand then. We found out later that the men who delivered us here were paid more for the pretty girls, and now we understand why. Those of us who were more pretty were the ones used in those parties."

Just then, the other Carmen chimed in. "I was not one of the pretty girls in my village. When Carmen told me what was happening at those parties, it was the first time in my life that I was happy not to be pretty."

"Well, I think you're pretty, Carmen. But you were just lucky not to be chosen," Lucy said to the other Carmen in Spanish.

She smiled. "Thank you, Miss Lucy. But can I tell you what happened on my boat? I was on the same big boat as my friend, but I was in a different small boat."

"Oh, please, Carmen, yes, we want to learn as much as possible," said Lucy.

"On my boat, most of us came from a village in Nicaragua, which was on the ocean. We did not land at the same place as my friend, Carmen here, but we also had to jump into the ocean and swim. Because we all said we had been swimmers, they did not give us any wood to help us, but we all made it to shore, though some became sick from swallowing seawater.

"We had three girls in each car, and we drove a long time to a place along the road that had toilets. The men gave each one of us a towel and told us to clean up and use the toilet. When we got back into the cars, they gave us bread and cooked fish, and we each got a bottle of water. They told us not to drink very much because we would not stop very often.

"I think we drove more than two days, only stopping when one of the two men needed the toilet. They kept taking more cooked fish and bread from a box in the trunk, but never more than two bottles of water each day. The men spoke mostly in English, so we weren't sure where we were going. Finally, on the third day, we came to this place."

"Yes, that is almost how it was for our car," Carmen said. "But instead of fish, they gave us cold sausages. One of the girls in my car needed to pee more often, but the men did not want to stop. When the girl begged them to stop, not wanting to pee in the car, one of the men hit her when we stopped. The other man yelled at him in Spanish, 'They don't pay as much for the damaged ones.'"

"I imagine that you started to see that things were not like the man back home had promised?" Liz asked, through Lucy's interpretation.

"I was becoming worried," Carmen said.

"Ask the girls how long they've been here?" Liz said to Lucy.

Carmen answered, "I'm starting to learn some English. It will be two years next month." "Were there other girls here when you arrived?" Liz asked.

Carmen needed some help from Lucy, but answered in English, "Maybe only 20. Our group was 16, and the others have come, sometimes 10 or 20 each month."

"And what was it like, staying here in this building?" Lucy asked.

"The food was terrible!" both girls said. "The meat was old, and we soaked it in vinegar, so we didn't get sick."

"Did the women who worked here mistreat you?" Liz wanted to know.

"They yelled a lot, but they didn't hurt us. But that nice lady, Camila, tried to keep the nasty ones away from us. Camila spoke Spanish and the other women only knew how to use nasty names in Spanish. We hated them," both Carmens said.

"Please ask them if they were treated well at the hotels, other than being used at those parties?" Liz asked Lucy.

Both girls said they were treated well by the head housekeepers. The other Carmen said she had spent her first year in the laundry, where she was also treated well. Both girls also said that the hotel staff would bring them sandwiches and milk when they could, and the girls always looked for good food on the Room Service trays when they cleaned the rooms.

"They are real survivors," Liz said to Lucy. "I really respect them."

Liz then asked Lucy to ask the girls about one of the girls named Lily. Emma Kowalski had described her as being different from the other girls.

"Lily worked in my hotel," Carmen said. "She came to many of those parties and she seemed to enjoy them. If one of the girls was not smiling, or not letting the men touch them, she would warn us in Spanish that we must do what they asked."

"How did Lily act if one of the girls was hurt by the men?" Liz wanted to know.

"Lily would tell the man at the hotel who planned those parties, if one of the girls had not been friendly. That man punished them by making them work double shifts, no lunch breaks, and still doing more parties. One girl fainted at work and the bus came to take her away. When we got back to the prison, that girl's bed was empty, and we never saw her again."

24

LIZ REPORTS PROGRESS

Liz went out to the makeshift FBI office they had set up on the first floor of the barracks and spoke to the young woman handling phone calls from irate customers. Most of them were wondering where their workers had disappeared to. Liz asked to speak to Sal Dominico.

The young lady pointed to a door and motioned Liz to go in. Liz knocked.

"I'm here. Come on in," she heard Sal say.

Liz opened the door and entered the small office space where Sal was sitting behind a folding table and chair.

"Hi, Sal. It looks like we have a real project on our hands, doesn't it?" Liz said.

"Busy, busy, Liz. But I'll tell you, this is what it was all about. Getting those dirt-bags in jail, and helping these girls get back to having a real life is very rewarding. I heard that you and Lucy were interviewing a couple girls. What was that about?"

"Lucy wanted to talk to the lady she met at that party. The one that caught her attention to possible trafficking. I think we got some really good intel from our conversation. I think one of the girls may have died at work while being punished with double shifts and lack of nourishment. The other thing that came out of our talk was that Lily, the girl I called 'the bottom' in our early discussions, is probably a professional prostitute. She was reprimanding girls at those parties if they didn't cooperate. If she hasn't been interviewed yet, I'd like to be in that interview."

'I think she may have been interviewed already, but with this new intel, I think a second interview is warranted. I'll arrange it to have one of my Agents and yourself in that second one." "Otherwise, how are things shaping up, Sal? Have those immigration attorneys had any input so far?"

"I was worried that they'd be a real pain, but Mrs. Kowalski must have prepped them well. Both attorneys said they did not want to seek asylum for criminals or those professionals outside of town, in that motel. I've asked INS to assess each one of the women and make recommendations."

"Lucy and I also had these two girls describe the process of how they were recruited and then how they were transported from Central America to this location. They were forced to swim ashore through the surf, somewhere along the Texas or Louisiana coast. They know that one of the girls in their group didn't make it, but there may have been more. The best they gave them for flotation was a piece of wood. They had three girls and two male drivers in each car, and they saw money exchanged at each delivery point. The men were aware of the girls' fate because they argued over who was getting the prettiest ones because they would get more money for them."

"I doubt that we will ever find most of those middlemen, but we had two carloads delivered this week with six new girls," Sal said. "Those drivers were arrested, and we hope to get some good intel from them. I guess they were in transit and hadn't heard about Trevor and the judge being arrested. I just can't wait to see that retired judge go to trial. I'm praying that he gets a feisty woman, U.S. Attorney trying his case. I found out he was already living well before getting involved with this business. The greedy bastard deserves to rot in Federal Prison."

"It is frustrating that many of the traffickers will not be found. Were you able to find anything in the files at the Trainor's office?" Liz asked.

"They used a lot of codes and nicknames for those they paid in cash. One of the guys who drove girls up here was called Gator-Boy in the files. It looks like they were being paid $1000 per girl, and $1500 for those with a 'P' in the description. The record would read, 'Gator-Boy, 2-F & 1-PF, $3500.' We suspected the meaning, but after hearing what your two interviewees told you, they were paying that extra $500 for the pretty ones."

How were the fishing boats and the recruiter in Central America paid?" Liz asked.

"We saw larger cash payments made to people in Louisiana and Texas. It looks like the Trainor guys were sending money to them to make payments to those transporters. Again, nothing but code names were used. We could visit those coastal villages in Mexico, but the Mexican Government is not cooperating. Those may be dead ends without the real names of those involved. Ask your girls if they saw any names on the boats. However, just like in the drug smuggling cases, the boat owners usually tie a piece of wood over the name."

"I spent most of my adult life dealing with girls treated worse than livestock," Liz said. "But I've never gotten over being sickened by things like this. I can almost understand the mentality of the men who pay to use these girls, though not condoning it. But the men who import women in the holds of fishing boats or cargo containers, not caring that some die in transit, and then hold them in a place like this 'prison,' as it seems the girls call it, is impossible for me to understand. I know we will prosecute some, but I don't think the punishment is severe enough. Carmen, the one from Guatemala, was just sixteen when she was brought here. She's about to turn eighteen, and knows nothing but pain in her life."

"Understood, Liz. But we need to keep on! By the way, I hope that Lucy understands what a great thing she is responsible for starting, not to mention disrupting her life to help us by going undercover. If it wasn't for Lucy, this operation could have gone on much longer, and now that you've told me that a girl died somehow while working at a hotel, we will start an investigation into that event. Please tell young Carmen that we'd like to speak with her about that."

"Yes, I'd like to find the person responsible for her apparent death. If the girl died, I wonder what happened to her body. Carmen said she never came back here, and that her bed was stripped. I remember what happened to the Moldovan girl who died in that house with the Chinese girls. She was found buried under a flower bed behind that house."

Sal took off his cap and scratched his head and then just as quickly, put the cap back on his head. "I'll have a cadaver dog brought in to search the property," he said.

"Thanks, Sal. If we can find evidence of deaths, then we can look for those responsible. We can at least justify manslaughter charges if not Murder 2."

"I'll call Pittsburgh to have them send a dog. Maybe Lucy can help that team by getting more details from Carmen. If Carmen or one of the other girls noticed activity on the property that may have involved digging holes or planting trees, we can start looking there."

"I'm sure that Carmen will be happy to cooperate. I'll let her know. I think we may also want to talk with the nice caretaker, Camila. She could have noticed them digging a grave."

25

LILY

Lily was one of the trafficked girls, but somehow, she had endeared herself to one of the traffickers. She spied on the other girls and reported any problems to someone in the traffickers' organization. Both Liz and Lucy asked if they could sit in on her second round of questioning. It took very little to get Lily talking, and in fact, she seemed to show sincere concern for what would happen to the other "prisoners" as Lily referred to them. As Liz had stated during her meeting at Emma's home, Lily started no different from the others. She only reported to the traffickers to protect herself.

It turned out that the person who Lily reported to was Lydia, but her extra "perks" actually came from Duncan. Duncan spoke some Spanish and he would take Lily home with him several times each month. For her duties as their spy, Lily was able to spend a few nights in luxury, eat nice meals, and of course, provide sexual favors for Duncan.

Because Lily repeatedly asked about what would happen to "her girls," as she referred to them, Lucy asked to consult with Liz and the interviewer in private. Outside the room,

Lucy asked, "Remember what you said about the "bottom" girl just being one of them, Liz? I had doubted that, but now, hearing Lily's repeated concern for what will happen to the others, I'm convinced that her concern is sincere.

She has not asked what will happen to her, but just the others." Then directing her question to the Spanish-speaking interviewer, "Do you hear her concern like I do?"

Elena, the interviewer, responded, "I didn't know this history before, and I'm unfamiliar with the bottom term, but I certainly saw the concern she seems to have for the other girls."

So, Lucy continued, "My question for you, Liz, am I crazy for thinking that Lily could be a great resource in trying to decide how each girl should be handled? I think Lily and possibly Camila could work together, telling us what each girl wants to do, and what their specific problems may be."

Liz responded, "Wow! I'm so glad we had you in the room. My minimal Spanish didn't pick up on that but seeing that both of you Spanish speakers agree on hearing that from Lily, I think it would be a great idea. So far, it doesn't appear that Lily has any criminal involvement, and if that is the case, using her detailed knowledge of these women would be extremely helpful. I'll run this idea past the FBI and the Social Services people who are working with the girls."

Based upon Lily's concern for the other girls' futures, she worked with Camila and Emma to determine which girls wanted to be considered for asylum. When that process was over, Lily asked to return to her home in Nicaragua.

26

THE RESULTS

Liz's team of Spanish-speaking volunteers, and the personnel brought in by the INS and FBI, interviewed each woman individually. Some were so nervous that they allowed one of the women who had already been interviewed to sit in with the nervous individual, but they were instructed not to coach them with answering questions. Those who were already identified as having been used for sex parties, due to the Red-Xs on their timecards, were interviewed with an extra woman, recommended by Beth Thomlinson, the young woman Liz knew from the Rescue Center. Beth had come from an abusive home and had

been trafficked to a small motel, where many of the girls were being sold for sex to transient workers.

Beth knew from her own experience and her work at the Rescue Center, that having an understanding, compassionate person involved was important for abused women.

The six women housed at the small, rural motel had been recruited as experienced prostitutes when they were trafficked. Three other women at other hotels were also found to be aware of their role in that capacity, and it was determined that they were not interested in finding a different profession. Those nine abductees were recommended for deportation back to their home countries.

Thirty-two others were found to have been used at the hotels' sex parties, and determined to have been unwilling participants, cooperating due to threats of physical punishment. Beth's Spanish-speaking volunteer was able to determine that six of those women wished to return to their homes in their native countries. However, the rest of those sexually abused women were traumatized and afraid to return home. The youngest of those women was sixteen but had been abducted at age 14.

The remainder of the women had been used exclusively as housekeepers, laundry staff, and cleaners in the kitchens and public areas. Nearly two-thirds of those women wanted to return to their home countries, being very disillusioned about what they thought was the American dream.

That left the twenty-eight who had been sexually abused and thirty others who were going to be considered for asylum. At that point, Emma Kowalski was contacted by Liz Trent and asked if she would contact her immigration attorneys, to help evaluate those who did not want to return to their homes.

Liz and Beth instructed the interviewers to try to identify the women who were cooperating with the traffickers, such as Lily, the one identified by Emma Kowalski, who Emma noted as being feared by the other girls. Lily may not have started out being cooperative, but she realized that she would get special treatment if she spied on the other girls. That didn't make her a bad person, but she would never be trusted by the other girls. Camila, the lady who had worked at the barracks, was instrumental in identifying the girls who were not trusted by the others, and Camila also helped with many of the interviews.

Emma Kowalski and Camila became friends through this process, and they were determined to find a way to keep the rescued girls employed if they were granted asylum. With the hotels now in desperate need of employees in their laundry, housekeeping, and cleaning staff, Emma approached the hotels and offered to start a new, legitimate company offering janitorial services. After all, her employees would have already been trained for the jobs they would be taking. In addition, Beth at the Rescue Center had been approached by several nursing homes after this event was covered by the local news agencies. The nursing homes were desperate to find help caring for their patients, and they were willing to offer the necessary training.

Emma approached the FBI and asked what would happen to the old factory building, where the girls had lived. The building had been slated for demolition by the City until Trainor purchased it. With the promise of housing a new thriving business in Erie, the City was able to arrange loans with several local banks to refurbish the interior with small rooms, good bathroom facilities, and a fully equipped galley, including adequate refrigeration and cooking equipment.

Emma's husband worked in the trades, and he was able to get volunteers for carpenters, plumbers, and electricians, to reduce the size of the bank loan needed for the refurbishment.

PROSECUTION

As expected, Trevor and the four businessmen who were identified as the business owners of Trainor Labor, refused to implicate any of the people they had paid to abduct and illegally transport these women into the United States. The five men were prosecuted and found guilty. Although many of the girls were underage and sexually abused, which could result in life sentences, their lawyer argued that

these women were not American citizens, and their clients were not aware of them being used for sexual purposes. Those four each received a 20-year sentence.

Trevor on the other hand, received a 40-year sentence because Lucy testified that Trevor knew about the Red Xs on those timecards, which the hotels used to signify that they had been sold for sex. Some of the hotel workers also testified that Trevor had discussed the Red-Xs with them and that they had paid extra in cash for those services. Trevor only avoided a life sentence because it could not be proven that he knew that some of the girls were minors.

Gabriel and three other hotel workers were also prosecuted, even though others were suspected of involvement in the sex trade. The cover-up that occurred after the arrest of Trevor was very thorough, and even though hotel managers were involved, they were able to hush up those who knew what was happening. Gabriel received a 20-year sentence as well as two others, and the last one only received a 7-year sentence. Young Tonia at the Countryside Inn was a witness in Gabriel's trial. The hotel owners were found to be not aware of what was happening at their hotel, but they quickly asked Tonia to take over as their manager.

Izzy's friend, Duncan Edwards, the Banquet Manager at the Fiesta Bay Hotel, was arrested at his home on the morning of the sting. The FBI did not want to wait for him to come to work, believing he might have been a flight risk. It appeared that his nice home, expensive car, and other luxuries would have been difficult to justify for a middle-management job since he was paying both alimony and child support.

Under interrogation, after being read his Miranda rights, Duncan denied any knowledge of the sex parties he was accused of setting up for the hotel guests. However, once they told him they had witnesses who knew about his involvement with the injured girl who was returned to the barracks, and about her two friends who later disappeared, Duncan broke into tears. He admitted that the girl had died while he tried to find her medical assistance. The doctor who he had been bribing to occasionally care for some occasional "problems," as he called them, happened to be out of town, and the girl died before he could decide what else he could do for her. He revealed who the doctor was, and that doctor was then arrested and in-terrogated.

The Agent asked Duncan what he had done with the girl's body, and he said he had returned to the barracks and buried her in a shallow grave at the back of the property. When asked what happened to the other two girls who had disappeared af-ter they asked about their friend, Duncan said the girls started asking questions, so he just reported the situation to Trevor who said he'd take care of them. He had not heard anything else about them.

Duncan agreed to lead the investigators to the place where he had buried the girl. When they found her, they dug up her body and took it to the coroner's office for an autopsy. The investigators tried to obtain the names of the men who were now suspected of killing the young woman during a gang rape, but Duncan said that there were never any records kept of those parties and that all payments were made in cash.

During the search for that girl's body, the cadaver dog found a second grave. It was suspected that this was the girl who was being punished, and had passed out at one of the hotels during working hours. It was suspected that Lydia was responsible for burying her body, but Lydia denied it. The in-vestigation into her death continues, but may be impossible to prosecute.

Next, the investigators asked how those Red Xs appeared on the time sheets, which signified that the girls had been used in those sex parties. Duncan told them that Lydia was the per-son responsible for keeping the timecards for all of the girls. When Duncan or others told Lydia that some of the girls would be staying late to attend a party, Lydia placed a Red-X on the girl's timecard for that day. Then Lydia sent the timecards to Trevor. Trevor added up the number of Red-X's for each hotel for that week and the man organizing the parties had to pay him $300 for each X. The organizers kept the other $50 for themselves.

When asked about the higher payments charged for an overnight stay by one of the women, Duncan said that he seldom reported those to Trevor, but occasionally paid Trevor an additional $100, telling Trevor that only one overnight was requested that week.

Duncan went to trial in Erie since the death had occurred there. He was found guilty by the jury of selling girls for sex, illegal disposal of a dead body, and second-degree murder for the death of Amira Gomez, the woman who had died during one of Duncan's parties. Pennsylvania sentences people accused of that felony to life in prison, but Duncan's lawyer argued that Duncan had not intended that the girl be injured by those men, and they were the ones guilty of murder. The judge read a lengthy statement into the record, telling Duncan that his actions led to the death of an innocent 17-year-old girl, but since Duncan had not intended for the girl to die, he would sentence him to 20 years in prison.

Then there was Lydia, who at first was just thought to be mean, and treated the girls terribly. It was found that she was the one who called Duncan to come and take away the injured girl. She was also the one who kept the timecards. This fact tied her to the sex-for-sale side of the business. Although Lydia was certainly complicit in the death of Amira Gomez, there was no hard evidence to make those charges stick, but the prosecutor was able to get her for selling the girls for sex and she was given 8 years in prison.

28

TREVOR

With Trevor's day-to-day, first-hand operation of the Trainor Labor Company business, he was considered a high flight risk. The U.S. District Attorney in Pittsburgh asked for a $1 Million bail to be set and based on the evidence in the indictment, the judge agreed. Trevor was held in Erie for only a few days and was then transferred to a Pittsburgh Federal Detention Center. It took several days of intense questioning, but as the government investigators began to disclose the statements made by Duncan Edwards, Camila, and Lydia at the barracks, Rex Wilson at the small motel brothel, and others who were all accusing Trevor of his involvement, Trevor began to crack, and asked if he could "make a deal." Although the investigator didn't see much hope for leniency, due to Trevor's total disregard for the welfare of these girls, the Agent told Trevor that "cooperation can always be considered by the judge during sentencing."

Trevor admitted that he had given the two girls, who had questioned the disappearance of their friend who was injured at the party, to the transporter who was delivering new women to Trainor. He had told the transporter that he could have the girls for free, but just deliver them to a location far away from Erie. As for the injured girl, he had told Duncan to handle it and not to tell him the details. Trevor swore he did not know that the girl's body had been buried behind the barracks.

During Trevor's eventual jury trial, the jury found Trevor guilty of all charges, including the sale of women for sex (based upon Lucy's testimony) except for the charge of second-degree murder for the one girl who died. The judge showed no leniency and sentenced Trevor to 30 years in Federal Prison.

29

LUCY & ROB

After everything calmed down, Rob went back to college on his FBI scholarship. Lucy did go back to her retail sales job but only on a part-time basis. She had become good friends with Beth, the young lady at the Erie Women's Shelter, and was volunteering with the Spanish-speaking families who came to the shelter for assistance.

It took Lucy nearly six months to convince Rob to give up his apartment and move in with her. Rob kept saying that he wanted Lucy to be sure of their relationship, even though Lucy had been convinced ever since the day that Rob broke Gabriel's nose in that hotel manager's office.

BURT'S DEBRIEF

About three days after the sting operations that shut down the operations of the trafficking contractor in Erie, Burt called Lucy. He wanted them to meet for what he called a "debrief."

"You bet, Burt!" Lucy said in response to Burt's request.

"Could we gather the others and have a group meeting? I'm talking about Emma Kowalski, Izzy the Chef, and certainly Liz. I want to officially thank all of them for being great, responsible citizens," Burt said.

"That sounds like a great idea, Burt. I'd like to thank them myself. Without their cooperation, we'd have had suspicions without the great results we've had. Do you think we could also invite Sal Dominico? He'd be able to update the group on what has happened to the contractors and the others involved. Can I also add Rob to that list?"

"As long we don't jeopardize the employees in any way, that would be great. And yes, I'm sorry that I left Rob off that list. I haven't gotten to know him very well yet, but I've heard he's a great guy, and broke a nose defending you!"

Lucy chuckled. "Yes, Rob sure stood up for me, and he has now become a permanent part of my life. I'm still meeting with Sal to update him on the processing of the rescued girls. So let me ask him if anything is still considered confidential. As far as I know, the hotel employees have been deposed, so their jobs are no longer in jeopardy."

"Okay then. Run the idea by Dominico, and I'll talk it over with Liz. I'm looking forward to getting to know Rob. He sounds like my kind of guy," Burt said.

The next morning, Lucy met with Sal, Teresa, and Mattie, the INS lead on the operation, for one of their twice-weekly meetings. Because Lucy was fluent in Spanish and had some exposure to the rescued girls, particularly the ones who had been sold for those sex parties, the team felt that she could act as an advisor for the interviewers.

Lucy knocked on Sal Dominico's makeshift office door. The office had been set up in the old factory that was being used as the barracks or "prison" as the girls called it. Teresa and Mattie were already present when Lucy opened the door and stepped inside. The office was nothing fancy. In reality, it was just an old conference room that the original factory had used. The FBI just pulled some of the old desks, tables, and chairs from around the building to make it usable.

Sal wanted the team to work there so that the girls didn't have to be shuttled back and forth. "Good morning, Lucy," Sal said to Lucy when she entered and closed the door behind her.

"Good morning," Lucy replied, then she hugged Teresa.

"How are you holding up? I bet you didn't imagine that we were going to keep you this busy," Sal said to Lucy.

"I'm fine. This has been such a rewarding experience, I'm energized. Seeing these girls go from being traumatized and confused to now being hopeful about their futures has been such a great

experience. I also want to mention that Beth, the young girl from the Women's Rescue Center, has been such an asset in this process."

Teresa nodded in agreement.

"Beth has offered to be there when we interview one of the sexually abused women. Even with her limited Spanish skills, Beth can somehow console those women and give them hope. They look into each other's eyes and communicate. I've seen it happen many times, and it is mystical."

"Thank you for offering to help, and extend our thanks to Beth," Mattie said, finally chiming in.

"Thank you also for trusting me with this, Mattie. And Sal, thank you for convincing me to get involved with the investigation in the first place. How many people can look at their lives and say they have made a positive impact on so many young women's lives? This has been such a wonderful opportunity."

"Remember, none of this would have been possible if you hadn't seen what you saw and then decided to tell somebody about it," Teresa said. "Do you know that most people would have turned a blind eye to what you saw? Some would have ignored it because they were afraid, but many would have just felt like it was none of their business. Your conscience is responsible for saving 143 women from slavery."

"How many are we sending home, Mattie?" Lucy asked.

"Only six were deported for cause. That means they were considered professional prostitutes. We had nineteen others who opted to return home. The other 143 women have been offered employment in a legitimate company. It was Camila's idea. She asked Emma Kowalski to work with her to manage the company. They are negotiating to buy this property and

improve it with a proper kitchen and real beds with new mattresses and linens. The girls will be paid a fair wage and they will receive conversational English classes, taught by students from the university."

"What about Lily?" Lucy asked.

Mattie answered her saying, "She had originally asked to go back home to Nicaragua, but when the other girls saw her concern for their fair treatment, they convinced her to stay and work with them. I think the others recognized that Lily was being forced to spy on them, and they understood what those threats would cause her to do. Lily can be a good leader, and both Emma and Camila agree that she should stay if she is willing to work with them."

"Good," Lucy said. "I also got that feeling when we interviewed her. She was more concerned about the others than herself. If the others now understand her motives, I hope they can learn to trust her."

"Seeing you mentioned Emma and Camila, I wanted to ask Sal if we have reached a point in this investigation where we can plan a meeting. More like an informal get-together with some of our team. We can include people like Liz Trent, Burt Snyder, the hotel employees who assisted us, and of course, Rob Brankovic. If we won't jeopardize either the investigation or the hotel employees' jobs, I think we owe it to them to tell them what their cooperation has produced."

Sal responded, "I hadn't thought of that, Lucy, but I think that is a great idea. We could hold the get-together right here and show them the newly updated barracks, which I think is no longer a prison."

"Some of the girls are now calling it 'their private hotel' even though the upgrades are not near complete. How are Emma and Camila going to pay for all of the changes that they plan?" Lucy asked.

Sal said, "Well, the property was seized by the government because it was purchased using money from an illegal operation. We asked the City of Erie, and they said that the factory had been scheduled for condemnation before Trainor Labor bought it. So, the government saw that it was not a saleable property and they are negotiating to transfer ownership to Chicas Salvados Corporation. And with the promise of improvements and a thriving Janitorial Services business to show taxable income, the city has arranged with several local banks to provide loans for the purchase of the new kitchen, laundry, and bedding improvements. Several of the large hotels have also donated construction services for carpenters, plumbers, and electricians, once they understood that their managers had been involved with illegal activities in their hotels. I think the hotels also badly need these women back in their employ, so they are very willing to cooperate."

"Unbelievable!" said Lucy. "They will have a real job, decent income, a safe place to live, and possibly become citizens as they had originally hoped. Will they become citizens eventually, Mattie?"

"People granted asylum in the United States receive a residency status and after five years, they can apply for citizenship if they show they have been employed as a resident over those five years. With the employment situation being provided for them here, that should not be a problem. I also heard that after the publicity we received following this rescue and arrests of the Trainor staff, several local nursing homes have contacted the FBI, asking if any of the women have experience in caring for the elderly. In the culture of the countries where these women are from, caring for their older family members is part of their lives, so that may also provide another possibility for good jobs."

"Back to your question about getting all of those people together, Lucy. Let me know when you'd like to do that," Sal said, "and I'll ask my agent in charge to provide some refreshments. Non- alcoholic of course. My boss has said he wants to meet all of the people involved in this investigation, so here's his chance. This bust is a real feather in the Pittsburgh FBI Office's cap, so I think he'll find some extra money in the office's coffee fund."

Sounds wonderful," Lucy said. "I'll try to get it organized for next week."

The following week, Lucy was able to get all of the important people together for what Burt had termed a debrief. Sal related all of the facts about arrests and his agent in charge complimented everyone for the role they played in putting an end to the trafficking operation.

Then Emma and Camila explained what Chicas Salvados Corporation was planning to do for the rescued women. They would not only supply janitorial services at the same hotels where the women had worked for free but would also provide training for those who wanted to work in nursing homes.

Burt waited until everyone else had spoken, and then he asked, "What is the FBI going to do about those 'coyotes' who transported these young women from Mexico and elsewhere? If we don't stop them, they will just sell more young girls to illegal contractors, supplying slave labor to other hotels in other parts of the country. I don't think we've put much of a dent in their entire operation."

Sal was about to respond, but his boss stopped him. The agent in charge said, "I understand your frustrations, Burt. We have asked the Mexican authorities to intervene, but they are not willing to investigate what they term as 'rumored illegal transport' of women who agreed to go to the United States."

"I know what the Mexicans will say, but we know otherwise. These young girls were basically kidnapped under false pretenses, Burt said"

"We have protocols to follow, Mr. Snyder. I don't see any way to find and prosecute those transporters," the agent in charge responded.

"I understand that you arrested the drivers of two carloads of new girls who were being delivered before the arrests became public. Can you get me into the prison where they are being held, so that I can interview them?" Burt asked.

"We can try," Sal Dominico said before his boss could answer. Sal knew what Burt wanted

to do, and although it was not following FBI protocols, he knew that Burt's 'ger-er-done' attitude might work, if he talked to those transporters. Burt had a way of talking with those types of guys, getting them to say things that they would never provide in an interrogation.

Then Burt asked, "Have you found and prosecuted all of the hotel managers that knew about what was happening?"

"We followed up on every lead for which we had hard evidence to file charges. We must assume that some of the guilty hotel staff did a good job of keeping their name out of the records, and if no one comes forward with additional testimony to incriminate them. There is nothing we can do.

Burt said no more, but Sal saw the look in Burt's eyes, and understood that Burt would find a way to get those people punished.

Sal got an interview for Burt with the four men who were being held in the Pittsburgh Federal Detention Center. Two of the men were Mexican nationals, but two were just deckhands on a Louisiana shrimp boat. Those two guys were young and scared about going to an American prison. Burt asked them if they knew what was going to happen to the girls they had transported to Erie, and they seemed naïve enough to believe that they were just there to find a job. When Burt told them what was going on with the illegal operations that they were involved in, the men seemed genuinely shocked.

They said they were paid just $500 each to drive for this job, and they were reimbursed for food and gas.

Burt told the young men that he could get them a much lighter sentence if they cooperated and named the people who gave them the job, and the names of the boats used to bring the girls into the United States.

After getting the men to spill the names of their suppliers, Burt decided to take a long overdue vacation. He'd always wanted to see the Louisiana Bayous. He stayed in several small towns with a lot of fishermen, hung out in the bars, and talked to the locals. The news special he saw on TV one morning said that several shrimp boats were sinking in the area's harbors. Some were U.S. flags, but a number of them were also Mexican and Guatemalan vessels that had dropped their loads of shrimp at the local processing plants. Sources told the reporter they appeared to be disgruntled crew members causing the sinkings because the captains had gone ashore to get drunk and there was evidence of sabotage in all of the sinkings. Even the engines had been started, causing major mechanical damage when the engines were submerged. No suspects were found and several of the boat owners filed bankruptcy because they had insufficient insurance to cover the repairs.

Burt ended his vacation and went back to Erie with a smile on his face. He had a great vacation!

When Burt returned home, he continued his private investigations. He had his trusted informants, such as Fred at the Fiesta Bay, amongst others, and whenever he had reason to suspect some of the hotel managers were violating their hotel chain's policies, such as taking kick-backs from suppliers, anonymous reports of those violations were received by the hotel's Corporate Ethics Manager. After Corporate investigated the charges, many of those managers, who all seemed to have been involved in the use of those captive women, either lost their jobs or were demoted.

Bob Ojala is a 1962 graduate of Marinette Catholic Central and the author of 9 novels (books, five novels and four non-fiction) with two more to be released soon. After graduating, Bob then joined the Coast Guard, spending four years on Great Lakes icebreakers, before heading to college. He earned a BSE in Naval Architecture and Marine Engineering from the University of Michigan, Class of 1970. He also spent seventeen years with the American Bureau of Shipping, and seven and a half years with the U.S. Army Corps of Engineers. Bob also worked over thirty-five years in his own business (which does include the time while with the USACE). He is still active in marine surveying.

Bob is a Wisconsin native with Finnish roots. Having a father as a merchant mariner for thirty-two years gave Bob an interest in the maritime industry, but not the desire to be a sailor. While he always wanted to document his father's career as a sailor on the Great Lakes, he saw that it was important to document all of the Great Lakes sailors, not just one segment of the industry. Designing small passenger vessels, tugs, and barges as a Naval Architect, he found he enjoyed working in the shipyard with the workers more than sitting in the design office. When the opportunity came to join the American Bureau of Shipping, working as a field surveyor, inspecting ships and equipment going into shipbuilding, Bob thought this was what he was looking for!

Eventually, Bob started his own marine surveying and consulting business. Because Great Lakes clients were slow in changing loyalties, he traveled the world (over 70 countries at last count), surveying cruise ships, tankers, dry docks, and even some warships. He also investigated accidents, pollution incidents, and several accidental deaths.

His books try to show the differences, and probably some similarities, between Great Lakes and deep-sea sailors, and also describe the various segments of the Great Lakes: ore boats, car ferries, and tugboats. With this background, Bob felt that he could describe the life of these merchant mariners and compare the Great Lakes versus the deep-sea sailors with some accuracy.

Bob Ojala's books include:

- Autobiography of a Ship's Marine Surveyor
- World Travels & Adventures of a Ship's Marine Surveyor (Autobiographical, under revision)
- Sweetwater Sailors (non-fiction, real-life stories from Great Lakes mariners)
- Sweetwater Sailors – The Rest of the Story (Sailor's wives, Unusual Sailors, more Women Sailors, Marine Construction, Excursion Boat Captains)
- A Tugboater's Life (Contemporary Romance based upon Great Lakes Marine Construction)
- The Tugboater Family (stand-alone, but flowing characters from A Tugboater's Life)

- Crew's Ship Affairs (Life on a large cruise ship, BE-LOW the passenger decks)
- KIDNAPPED – A Tugboater's Tale (Human Trafficking in middle-America)
- Undercover again – Fighting Human Trafficking

In his novel, "Kidnapped: A Tugboater's Tale", the captain and her husband leave the tugboat to get pizzas for the crew and they are kidnapped by sex-traffickers. Bob explained the reason he has knowledge about human trafficking; he had the same training as active-duty Army soldiers while he worked with the Army Corps of Engineers. He was shocked to find out that human trafficking for "sexploitation" is worse in the United States than anywhere in the world. This story shows how the victims are lured, and the different ways they are controlled using violence, threats, and drugs but also ones who use kindness and brainwashing with the same results. It's an exciting and good read.

www.ingramcontent.com/pod-product-compliance
Lightning Source LLC
Chambersburg PA
CBHW071927150726
47999CB00001B/129